PUFFIN BOOKS

HI THERE, SUPERMOUSE!

Nicola was a rather straggly sort of person. She was tall for an eleven-year-old, and gangly with arms and legs that seemed too long for her body. Rose was short and bouncy with forget-me-not blue eyes and a round pink face full of freckles.

These two sisters not only look unrelated and have completely different temperaments, they also can't stand one another. Fuelled by her mother's ambitions since the age of four, Rose has had so many dancing and drama lessons that she's now convinced she's the greatest little actress since Shirley Temple. Nicola can only brood on the injustice of this situation. She knows that she can dance and act too, but no one's prepared to give her the chance – that is, until Rose falls ill and Nicola is asked to stand in for her.

A witty and perceptive story of family rivalry for readers of 9 to 12.

D0018975

JEAN URE

Hi There,
Supermouse!

Illustrated by Martin White

PUFFIN BOOKS

Puffin Books, Penguin Books Ltd, Harmondsworth, Middlesex, England
Viking Penguin Inc., 40 West 23 Street, New York, New York 10010, U.S.A.
Penguin Books Australia Ltd, Ringwood, Victoria, Australia
Penguin Books Canada Ltd, 2081 John Street, Markham, Ontario, Canada L3R 1B4
Penguin Books (N.Z.) Ltd, 182–190 Wairau Road, Auckland 10, New Zealand

First published by Hutchinson Junior Books Ltd 1983
Published in Puffin Books 1985

Copyright © Jean Ure, 1983
Illustrations copyright © Hutchinson Publishing Group, 1983
All rights reserved

Made and printed in Great Britain by
Richard Clay (The Chaucer Press) Ltd,
Bungay, Suffolk
Set in Baskerville

1

'*Honestly*, Nicola.' Mrs Bruce regarded her elder daughter with the exasperated air of one who has very nearly reached the end of her tether. 'I just don't know how you could *do* such a thing. I don't know how you *could*.'

Nicola shook her hair into her eyes and stared down glumly at the carpet through the lank strands of her fringe. She supposed she ought to say something, only what was there to say? The thing that she had done was so indisputably *awful* – and she hadn't even been aware that she was doing it until it was too late. One moment she had been sitting there, at the dining room table, struggling to write an essay about 'Getting up in the Morning' for Miss McMaster, on Monday; the next, to her horror, she had been busily drawing a face on the toe of one of her sister Rose's tap dancing shoes.

What made it even worse (if anything *could* make such an evil deed even worse) was that the shoes were red leather and very nearly new, and the pen she'd used for drawing was deep dark black and wouldn't come out no matter how much she spat on it, nor how hard she rubbed. In fact, she'd only succeeded in turning what had been a rather good face into a great splotchy mess. If she'd left it as a face, she could at least have done a second one to match. She might have started a new fashion, shoes with funny faces. *She* wouldn't mind if someone drew faces on her plimsolls, or her gum boots. But then, of course, she wasn't Rose. Rose was Rose,

and Rose was perfect. Rose was pretty. Rose was *good*. Rose couldn't go round with faces on her shoes.

Rose, at this moment, was screaming fit to bust. Nicola pushed her fringe back out of her eyes. Stupid cow. Making all that fuss over a mere shoe.

'Hush, now!' Mrs Bruce, distracted, pulled Rose towards her and stroked her hair with a soothing hand. Rose's hair was bright chestnut and springy: Nicola's was dark, and limp, and straggled. She was rather a straggly sort of person. She was tall, for an eleven-year-old, and at a gangly stage, where her arms and legs seemed too long for her body. Rose was short and bouncy, with forget-me-not blue eyes and a round pink face full of freckles. Nicola's face was thin, and rather sallow, and her eyes were brown, and deep set. Nobody would ever have taken them for sisters. There was only a year between them, but already Nicola was like a walking beanpole beside small, compact Rose. Their father, fondly, called Rose his little Rose Petal; Nicola, for almost as long as she could remember, had been 'old Nickers'. Sometimes she wished that he wouldn't, but mostly it didn't bother her. She knew that she was her father's favourite. Not that he loved her any more than he loved Rose; just that really and truly he had hoped for a boy, and everyone always said that Nicola was 'as good as'. Rose was her mother's favourite – Mrs Bruce didn't care for boys. She definitely loved Rose more than she loved Nicola. She looked at Nicola now, over Rose's copper curls, and said, 'How anyone could be so *wicked* . . .'

Rose wrenched her head away.

'She did it on purpose, just to be mean!'

'I did not!' Nicola was indignant. 'How was I to know it was your stupid shoe?'

'You could see it was my shoe! You only had to *look*.'

'Well, I didn't, and anyway it oughtn't to have been there . . . shoes on a *table*.'

7

'Don't be ridiculous, Nicola!' Mrs Bruce spoke sharply. 'It's no use trying to make excuses, you've ruined a perfectly good pair of shoes. I don't even know if it'll clean. They'll probably have to be dyed.'

A wail broke forth from Rose.

'I don't want them dyed! I want a new pair!'

'If she had the money, I'd make her pay for a new pair. As it is –' Mrs Bruce eyed Nicola, sternly '– you can certainly pay for any repair work that needs doing. And *that's* letting you off lightly. It's about time, my girl, that your father started to take a sterner line with you. I've had just about as much as I can stand. Ordinary naughtiness is one thing; but when it comes to deliberate acts of vandalism –'

'It wasn't!' Nicola felt impelled to speak up in her own defence, though she knew that it was hopeless. How could she expect her mother to understand, when she didn't even understand herself? She tried, nevertheless. 'It wasn't deliberate,' she said. 'It was an accident.'

Rose, in shrill tones, said, '*Accident?*'

Mrs Bruce only pursed her lips.

'Trying to wriggle out of it won't help, Nicola. This isn't the first time this sort of thing has happened. What about the other day, when you threw ink all over the place?'

'That *was* an accident.'

'Well, maybe it was, but this certainly wasn't. You can hardly pretend not to have known what you were doing.'

But I didn't, thought Nicola. I *didn't*. She looked down at her English rough book, still lying open on the table. She looked at what she had written:

'Getting up in the Morning. I get up in the morning at seven o'clock when my dad brings me a cup of tea. I get up straigt away because of taking my dog Ben round the block. My sister Rose dos'nt get up untill our mum's called her three times Rose its time to get up or you'll be late for school but even then she dosn't always come imedeately. If I didn't come I would be told I am lazy and slothfull and who is to take Ben for his walk, but my mum says Rose needs her sleep because of going to be a dancer and so it is alright for her to stay in bed late and –'

And what? wondered Nicola. What had she been going to write next? She couldn't remember. She couldn't remember anything. Had she *really* been wicked enough to draw a face on Rose's tap shoe?

The tap shoe, unhappily, told her that she had. It sat there on the table, squat and accusing, with two eyes, and a nose, and a downturned mouth which seemed to say, 'This really is not amusing, you know.'

'I didn't *mean* it,' said Nicola.

'It's all very well saying you didn't mean it, but the fact remains that you *did* it. Didn't you?' Nicola munched glumly at her bottom lip. Mrs Bruce shook her head. 'It's beyond me,' she said. 'It really is. If you were a stupid girl, I could understand it, but you're not. So why behave as if you were?'

Nicola said nothing: she was too busy trying to munch all the way down to her chin. If her teeth had been just a bit longer, or her chin just a little bit shorter . . .

'There's no point in being clever at school,' said Mrs Bruce, 'if you're going to be stupid outside it. There, now, Rose, love.' She pulled a handkerchief from her pocket. 'You have a good blow and dry your eyes. And don't worry about the shoes; we'll get something done. It might be quite exciting, having them dyed another colour . . . how about blue? Blue would be nice.'

Rose, hiccuping into the handkerchief, wept afresh and declared that no one, but *no one*, had blue tap shoes.

'Well, then! You can set a new trend, can't you? Nice bright blue, to match your eyes.'

'But what about this morning?' Rose almost shrieked it. 'What will Madam Paula say?'

'You'll just have to apologize to Madam Paula and explain that your elder sister –' Mrs Bruce rested a moment, significantly, on the word elder '– your *elder* sister, who ought to know better, thought it funny to deface other people's property.'

'I *didn't*,' said Nicola. 'I didn't *know*.'

Mrs Bruce ignored her. She picked up the one good shoe and the one bad shoe and thrust them gently at Rose.

'Off you go! You don't want to be late. Tell Madam Paula we're thinking of letting you have extra classes next term . . . that will please her. She's always saying you're one of her star pupils. As for you, Nicola, you can get out from under my feet and take that dog for a walk.'

'I've already taken him for one.'

'Then take him for another!'

'But I'm doing my *home*work. I've got an essay to write.'

'You can write it later. Go along! Do as you're told. Saturday morning and sitting about the place . . . go out and get some fresh air. Blow some of the naughtiness out of yourself – and don't go over that building site!'

There were two building sites in Fenning Road. There was one close by, which was the one her mother didn't like; and there was another further down which Mrs Bruce didn't yet know about because she always walked up towards the shops, in Streatham High Road, instead of down the other way, towards the Common. Nicola made a quite definite distinction in her mind between the two: between *that* building site (which had been forbidden) and the *other* building site (which hadn't). It couldn't possibly be termed disobedience to clamber over the earthmound into the *other* building site. She wasn't doing anything wrong. No one had put up any notices saying 'Private' or 'Trespassers will be prosecuted'. They hadn't even put up a fence. In any case, it was better for Ben, because there weren't any motorcars for him to get run over by.

The building site was full of mud. Back in the summer there had still been some grass, and even a few flowers, but now it was autumn, and the rain had come, and men with bulldozers had been at their work, carving trenches and throwing up mountains. On the whole, Nicola preferred it this way. It gave more scope. Trenches and mountains could be anything you cared to make them, from battlefields to lunar landscapes. Grass and flowers were too much like the local park, with its 'Dogs must be kept under control' and its 'Keep to the path' and its 'No entry'. And anyway, they made her think of Rose. Rose had green fingers. (Rose had *everything*.) She grew geraniums in pots and cultivated her own corner of the garden, so that sometimes, when he wasn't calling her Rose Petal, Mr Bruce referred to her as 'my little gardener'. Nicola hated gardening. The only part of it she enjoyed was stoking bonfires, and her mother wouldn't let her do that any more. She said she couldn't be trusted – all because she'd accidentally set light to the fence and Rose had gone running indoors screaming. Silly cow. Nicola stubbed her toe, viciously, into a pile of loose earth. Rose was so *stupid* – and she was a tell tale. 'Nicola's done this, Nicola's done that . . . Nicola's *hurt* me, Nicola's been *mean* to me . . . Nicola's *horrible*.' Well, and so could Rose be, when she wanted. She was just sly about it; always sucking up to people, putting on her airs and graces, prinking and preening – 'I'm little *Rose*mary, oh, aren't I *pretty* –'

Nicola, long-leggitty in black wool tights and a red plaid skirt that didn't reach her knees, did a little twirl, tiptoe in the mud.

'Such a *dear* little girl – such a *sweet* little girl –'

Prink, preen, simper, simper.

'Just *see* how she can point her toe! See her curtsy – see her pirouette –'

Nicola pirouetted vigorously on the top of her mud bank.

'*See her fall flat on her silly fat face* –'

BANG.

Slap, thud, into the mud.

'Nicola's *hurt* me, Nicola's been *mean* to me . . . boo hoo! Now I'm all *dirty* –'

Absorbed in being Rose, Nicola covered her face and roared, dramatically.

'Yes, and serve you jolly well *right*!'

With a demonic yell, she sprang off the mound. She was back again, now, to being Nicola.

'Silly, simpering, self-righteous *cow*!'

Whooping and hallooing, she danced around the mound.

'Serve her right, serve her right, serve her –'

'Excuse me!'

Nicola came to an abrupt halt, in the middle of a whoop. Outside, on the pavement, a lady was standing. She beckoned to Nicola, and nodded; Nicola scowled. The lady cupped a hand to her mouth.

'May I have a word with you?'

She didn't *sound* as if she was going to make a scene; still Nicola was wary. In her experience grown ups – even youngish, glamorous grown ups, like this one – only ever wanted to have words with you for one thing, and that was to tell you that what you were doing was something you ought not to be (such as playing on building sites). Nicola slouched across, reluctantly.

'I've seen you somewhere before,' said the lady. 'I'm trying to think where . . . do you by any chance have a big black dog?'

Unfortunately, just at that moment, Ben chose to put in an appearance. If he hadn't, she would have denied all knowledge. (It was always safer to deny all knowledge where Ben was concerned: you never knew what he might have got up to when you weren't looking.)

12

'That's the one!' said the lady.

Ben grinned, and wagged his tail.

'Is he yours?'

Since Ben, at that point, was sitting companionably on her toe, she couldn't very well disown him. She mumbled, 'Yes,' in a way that might be taken for 'no' if any accusations were to be made.

'Then that's where I've seen you!' The lady seemed pleased. (Because she had solved a mystery, or because she had tracked down a culprit?) 'Going into the house with the green shutters . . . I remember your dog trying to get a tree trunk through the gate with him and not succeeding! I live just there, by the way.'

She pointed to a large, ivy-clad house overlooking the building site. Nicola's scowl intensified. So what? It wasn't *her* building site. It didn't say 'Private'. It didn't say 'Trespassers will be –'

'Do you have dancing classes?' said the lady.

'No.' Nicola grabbed at Ben's collar, to prevent him going off again. He was already plastered in mud from one end of himself to the other. 'That's my sister does that,' she said. She wasn't taking the blame for anything Rose might have done. Not that Rose ever *did*.

'I was watching you,' said the lady. 'I thought perhaps you might have come in here secretly to practise.'

Nicola stood her ground.

'It doesn't say "Private",' she said.

'No, it doesn't, does it? Rather amazingly . . . they're usually terrified of a few stray children getting in and managing to enjoy themselves. After all –' she waved a slender hand at the sea of mud '– just think of all the damage you could cause . . . what's your name, by the way?'

'Nicola Bruce,' said Nicola. Now she supposed there was going to be a complaint made, like the time she'd been caught climbing on the roof of the girls' lavatory at school.

She hadn't been doing any *harm*. What harm could you do to a lavatory? *Or* a mouldy building site. It was stupid to say, 'Think of all the damage you could cause.' Nobody could cause damage to a bit of bare earth. It wasn't as if there was anything growing in it.

'Well, I'll say goodbye, then, Nicola. I expect we'll bump into each other again. Mind you don't get mud all over that pretty skirt!'

The lady turned, and walked off up the road, in the direction of the shops. She was tall and slim, in red velvet jacket and trousers. From behind, she looked almost like a boy. Quite often, when she was wearing jeans, people said that Nicola looked like a boy. That was one of the reasons why Mrs Bruce wouldn't let her wear them very often; not only because she didn't like boys, but because she believed that girls should be girls. Rose was always a girl. Whenever she was taken to buy a new frock she inevitably chose something soft and frilly that would have made Nicola look like a piece of twig dressed up as a sugar plum fairy. Rose just *naturally* looked like a sugar plum fairy.

Nicola tossed her head. So, who cared? She certainly didn't. She had better things in life to worry about than stupid clothes. She let go Ben's collar and he went hurtling off, joyously, through a trench full of dirty water. Nicola stomped back again to her mound.

'Look at *me* – I am *Rose* . . . Sugar Plum Fairy with a big red nose . . .'

She wished that grown ups would mind their own business. It just wasn't the same, when you knew that they were spying on you.

2

Nicola had forgotten all about the lady on the building site. A whole week had passed, and other things had happened in the meantime. Miss McMaster had praised her essay on 'Getting up in the Morning'. She had given her eight out of ten and read it aloud to the class as an example of a good piece of writing – 'even if it does dwell rather obsessively on your sister Rose *not* getting up'. Now she had given them another essay to write, on the subject of 'My Family'. Nicola had already composed the opening paragraph:

'My Family. My family is made up of my mum and dad and my sister Rose. There is also my dog Ben. My mum and dad sleep in the front bedroom in a large bed with a blue cover. My sister Rose sleeps in the backbedroom wich is the next biggest becuase she has to have spase for all her dansing things and to practise pleeays' (she wasn't too sure about this word) 'before she goes to bed wich means I have to have the very smallest room of all scarsely any bigger than a cuboard in wich to put myself and my belongings wich I have quite a number of.'

That had been on Wednesday. On Thursday Rose had come back all cock-a-whoop from her ballet class saying that Madame Paula had said she would be ready to go on point next term and please, *please* could she go out and buy a pair of point shoes straight away, so as to have plenty of time in which to darn them and sew on ribbons? To Nicola's disgust, Mrs Bruce had said that she might just as well, since 'sure as eggs' the price would only go shooting up if they waited. She hadn't said that when Nicola had wanted a pair of running shoes. She hadn't said anything at all about the price of running shoes shooting up. She'd simply said that 'You'd better wait and see what Christmas brings.' She'd been quite cross when Nicola reminded her of it.

'There's a world of difference between shoes for ballet and shoes for running. If Rose is going to be a dancer, then she needs the right things. *You* can run in your plimsolls. In any case, I should have thought the less said on the subject of shoes the better, as far as you were concerned.'

In the end, she had relented and said that if Nicola could manage to keep herself out of trouble for just forty-eight hours, then maybe – 'I said *maybe*' – she would reconsider. It was now three o'clock on Saturday afternoon and Nicola hadn't done anything wrong since half-past seven on Thursday evening. That meant she had kept out of trouble for forty-three hours and thirty minutes. (She was ticking it off in a special notebook by the side of her bed.) Nothing, surely, could go wrong *now?*

She had forgotten about the lady from the building site – at least, not so much forgotten as dismissed her from her mind. After all, if she had been going to make a complaint, she would have done it ages ago. Nobody stored up grudges for a whole week; or did they?

Did they?

The front gate had been pushed open. Nicola heard it as she sat perched on her bedroom windowsill constructing a model Concorde from a model kit. Her bedroom windowsill was triangular in shape and wide enough for her to curl up on. If she peered out of the left-hand window she could just make out the porch over the front door and, if she was quick enough, see who it was coming up the path. She peered – and recoiled in haste. Not only in haste, but indignation, as well: it was the lady from the building site.

16

She was wearing a skirt, instead of the red trousers, and her blond hair was loose about her shoulders instead of being scraped back from her head as it had been before, but Nicola had no difficulty in recognizing her. She had the sort of face that wasn't easy to forget. It was bony, like a model's, and very pale, except for the eyes, which were huge and long-lashed with green sparkly stuff over the lids. In other circumstances, Nicola might have been impressed. All she felt now was a sense of outrage. To have waited a whole *week* –

The doorbell rang. In a flash, Nicola was out of her room and along the landing. As she reached the head of the stairs a door opened somewhere below and her mother came into view, wiping her hands on a towel as she trod across the hallway. Nicola crouched, spiderlike, at her post. She watched as her mother opened the front door. Almost at once, she heard the light, crisp voice of the lady from the building site, 'Mrs Bruce? I do apologize for calling round unannounced! My name is Pamela French – I live just down the road. Number ninety-eight. I wondered if I might have a word with you about Nicola?'

'Nicola?' said Mrs Bruce. Her voice was guarded. 'What did you want to –?'

'I was watching her, last Saturday. I was really on my way to do some shopping, but I just had to stop. She was over on the building site – you know the one? Where the old hotel used to be? It's right next door to us, as a matter of fact. Anyway, she was dancing around, as children do, and I couldn't help noticing –'

'Miss French.' Mrs Bruce breathed, rather deeply. Nicola could imagine how her forehead would be puckering. '*Mrs* French, I beg your pardon . . . I think I'd rather like you to come inside and say what you have to say in front of Nicola's father, if you don't mind. If it wouldn't be putting you to too much trouble?'

'Oh! No, not at all.' Pamela French sounded surprised.

She also sounded quite pleased. (How mean could you get? thought Nicola.) 'I'd be only too glad to.'

Nicola watched, with bitterness at heart, as her mother led the way across the hall and into the sitting room. She heard her say, 'Norman, this is Mrs French –' and then the door closed and all sound was cut off. Inch by inch, she squirmed her way down the stairs. It was a trick she'd learnt in the past; if you sat on the very bottom step and leaned as far forward as you possibly could, and provided the television wasn't turned on, you could hear almost every word that people were saying. Even if anyone came out when you weren't expecting it you weren't likely to be caught, because the banisters were the filled-in sort and gave perfect cover for a quick scamper back to safety. Rose had once informed her, in her goody-goody way, that it was a sin to eavesdrop, but Nicola didn't see why it should be. It didn't say anything about it in the Bible. They'd had to learn all the ten commandments by heart for RI last term, and there' hadn't been a single thing about Thou Shalt Not Eavesdrop. They'd have said, if it was a sin. Anyway, she didn't care if it was or it wasn't. People *oughtn't* to talk about you behind your back. It was only an excuse for saying horrid things.

Nicola reached the bottom step and carefully lowered herself on to it. Mr Bruce usually had the television turned on, for the sport, on a Saturday afternoon, but obviously he'd been made to turn it off, because she heard her mother's voice quite distinctly, '*Nicola?* You want *Nicola?*'

'If you think that she'd enjoy it – which I'm sure she would, if the way she was dancing around was anything to go by.' (That was Pamela French.) 'I've never seen a child so absorbed! It was quite magic to watch.'

'But *Nicola* –'

'What exactly –' Mr Bruce joined in the conversation '– what exactly would you want her to do?'

'Let me explain . . . I belong to this little group called "The Silent Theatre". It's what you might call semi-professional. We don't perform for money, but we've most of us been in the business at one time or another –'

'Business?' said Mr Bruce.

'On the stage.' His wife sounded impatient. She knew more about such matters than he did. 'Dancing, acting . . . that sort of thing.'

'Yes, that's right. A couple of us used to be actresses, I used to be a dancer, Ted – that's the man who runs the group – used to be a professional mime. We try to set our standards as high as possible. That's why, when I saw Nicola –'

'But Nicola can't dance!'

'Actually, I think she probably could, but in any case we don't really need a dancer. We just need a child who's expressive and can move well. What we do, you see, is put on little shows in mime and take them round to the old folks' homes and the hospitals – schools, orphanages – places like that. We've already got one planned for Christmas, which we're in the middle of rehearsing, but the trouble is we're short of a child. It's just for the one sketch – "The Family Portrait". It's great fun, I'm sure Nicola would enjoy it. It's all about this Victorian family sitting for their photograph. What we want Nicola for is the Bad Little Girl . . . we've got a Good Little Boy, but we just can't find a Bad Little Girl anywhere. I've been keeping my eyes peeled for weeks. We did have one, only her family suddenly moved out to Australia, which left us rather in the lurch.'

'But you can't possibly want *Nicola*.' Mrs Bruce had recovered herself. Her voice was firm. 'Rose is the one you want. She's our little dancer.'

'Yes, Nicola said her sister took dancing lessons.'

'Rose will be only too happy to do it for you. Can't get enough of it, that one. Dancing all the day long . . . up on

20

her toes ever since she was a tiny tot. It's a pity she's not here just at the moment, or you could see for yourself.'

'Yes! I'm sure. The only thing is –'

'I'd have kept her in, if I'd known you were coming. Unfortunately, she won't be back for another hour or so. She's gone off with a friend to watch an old Fred Astaire movie. Would you believe it? He's her idol. Fred Astaire! You'd think he was a pop star, the way she carries on . . . let me show you a photograph of her. Here . . . this is Rose.'

Rose, Rose, up on her toes,

Overbalanced by her big red nose . . .

'This is when she had her first ballet dress – that's her in the school play – that's the show they put on last term at dancing school – and that one was taken just a couple of weeks ago, on her birthday.'

'Ah –' Even crouched on the stairs, Nicola could detect a certain lack of enthusiasm in the response. Her heart began to warm to Pamela French. Perhaps, after all, not *every*body thought that Rose was wonderful. 'Yes . . . she's rather a – a *pretty* little girl, isn't she?'

'Oh, she's got the looks.' That was Mr Bruce. He was proud of the way Rose looked. Rose took after her mother, who had been what Mr Bruce called 'a stunner' before she had had two children and grown plump. Nicola was more like her father, dark and wiry. 'Interesting,' people said, when they wanted to be kind. 'Yes, she's a charmer, all right.' Nicola could see him shaking his head, with an air of satisfaction. 'No denying that.'

'That's the only thing that worries me, you see.' Pamela French spoke earnestly. 'If it was a *good* little girl that we were after – but it's a bad one we want! Nicola struck me as exactly the right type. I can just imagine Nicola being into all *sorts* of mischief.'

Mr Bruce chuckled.

'You can say that again! Drives her mother to distraction,

the things she gets up to.'

'That's *precisely* the sort of child we want! Full of naughtiness, full of high spirits –'

'Rose is full of high spirits.' Mrs Bruce was plainly nettled. 'You couldn't get anyone more high-spirited than Rose.'

'But is she full of natural wickedness?'

'She could act it – she's a lovely little actress. She nearly got a part in *Annie* last year. She got through the first audition. She was called back. It was a very close run thing. Besides –' Mrs Bruce hammered home the final nail in the coffin '– Nicola's not reliable. She gets these fads and fancies . . . nothing ever lasts more than five minutes. You'd find she just wouldn't bother to turn up, or she'd roll in half an hour late. As for learning lines . . .'

'Oh, but there aren't any lines, Mrs Bruce! It's all in mime.'

'Well, there you are . . . what does Nicola know about that sort of thing? She's never done anything like it in her life. Rose, now, has been at it since she was a toddler. Since she was four years old. You can rely on Rose. Nicola, I just wouldn't answer for. She's got no staying power, that's Nicola's trouble. In any case, it would be inviting disaster . . . she can't even walk across a room without tripping over her feet! No, Mrs French. I wouldn't be happy, foisting Nicola on to you. Rose is the one you want. Suppose I ask her to pop round and see you when she gets in? That way you could tell her all about it – work out when she'd be wanted for rehearsals, and so on. I'm sure Madame Paula wouldn't mind her missing the occasional class, if it's in a good cause. You'll find her very professional. Very conscientious. She's had a lot of experience . . . you needn't worry that Rose will let you down.'

'Well . . . what can I say?'

Pamela French seemed at a loss. Nicola, still curled into a tight knot on the bottom step, dug her fingernails hard into the palms of her hands.

Don't let her say yes. Don't let her say yes. Don't let her say –

'I suppose I shall have to bow to your judgement . . . if Rose is the family performer –'

'You won't regret it. Not with Rose. I can vouch for her. What time shall I tell her to come round? Five o'clock? Would that be convenient?'

'Yes, by all means. Five o'clock would be fine. I'll look forward to seeing her.'

'What number was it again? Number –'

The sitting room door opened and her mother appeared. Nicola didn't wait to hear any more: she fled back upstairs, monkeylike, on all fours. There was a general buzz of conversation, then the front door clicked, and from her bedroom window she could see Pamela French walking down the path towards the gate. The front door clicked again, and was shut.

For a second there was silence; then a volley of sound burst forth from the sitting room: her father had obviously turned the television on again. In spite of it, she heard her mother's voice quite clearly, 'Imagine that! Wanting *Nicola* . . .'

3

'Mrs French,' said Rose, 'used to be with the Royal Ballet.'

'Mrs French,' said Nicola, 'used to be with the Royal Ballet . . .' She said it in a high-pitched squeak, which was meant to be an imitation of Rose. She was sick of hearing Rose go on about Mrs French. Mrs French this, Mrs French that . . . Mrs *French* says I'm a natural. Mrs *French* says I've got rhythm. Mrs *French* –

'She used to be a soloist,' said Rose.

'So what?' Nicola swung her bag full of school books and caught a passer-by a sharp blow upon the shin. The passer-by turned, and looked at her, irritably. Passers-by always did look at Nicola irritably. There just seemed to be something about her which annoyed people.

'Being a *soloist*,' said Rose. 'With the Royal *Ballet*.'

'Big deal.'

'Some people never get out of the corps. I wouldn't stay if I was always going to be in the corps. Mrs French says there isn't much danger of it . . . she says I've got too much personality. She says –'

I'll kill her, thought Nicola. If she says it once more, I shall *kill* her.

'She says people with strong personalities don't merge well. She says –'

I don't care what she says. What she says is piffle. Piffle and rubbish and *junk*. I shan't listen to it. I shall close my ears and think of something else.

All very well, but it wasn't that easy; not with Rose prattling nineteen to the dozen at her side. Rose had been unbearable, this last couple of weeks. Ever since she'd been given the part – *Nicola's* part – she'd been like a cat that had got at the cream. Even Madame Paula had faded into insignificance. Now it was all Mrs French and rehearsal schedules and 'being called'.

'I've been called for next Tuesday . . . I've been called for Sunday morning . . .'

Nicola scowled. She slung her bag of books over her shoulder. It should have been her that was being called – it should have been *her* doing the part. She bet she could do it just as well as Rose. She'd watched her, at home, showing her mother how it went. 'We all come in like *this*, and then I have to do *this*, and then Mama shakes her finger at me, like *this*, and then –' And then she had to pull a rude face, which was something that Rose couldn't do. Rose didn't know how to pull faces – not real, wicked, ugly faces. Rose only knew how to screw up her nose and look pretty. Nicola couldn't look pretty to save her life, but she did know how to pull a good face. She knew exactly how she would have done it, if she had been given the part. She'd practised it, in secret, in front of the bathroom mirror, sticking out her tongue and making her eyes go all squinty so that she looked like one of the gargoyles on the roof of the local church. That was how it *ought* to look; not all simpering and soppy, as Rose did it.

Rose was now skipping along the pavement, getting under people's feet as they tried to do their last-minute shopping. She had been 'called' for seven o'clock that evening, which made her even more unbearable than usual. She was only doing it to show off. She liked people to stop and watch – she fondly imagined that they were all thinking how wonderful she was. Nicola's bet was that some people were thinking how stupid she looked. Skippity-hopping about the place. She wished just *one* person would say

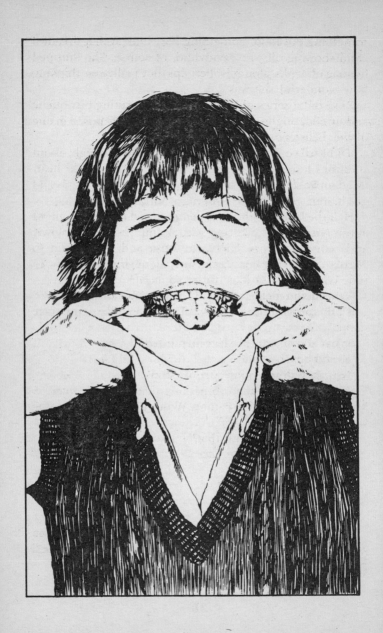

something out loud. Something like, look at that dreadful child showing off. . . Nobody did, of course. She humped her bag of books, gloomily. Perhaps they really *were* thinking how wonderful she was.

Rose did a series of little twirls past a waiting bus queue and turned, bright-eyed, with her feet carefully posed in one of her ballet positions, to wait for Nicola.

'Did I tell you?' Her voice rang out, shrill and high, about six times louder than usual, so that everyone could hear. 'Madam Paula's got me an audition for *The March Girls*. . . if I get it, I'm going to be Rosemary Vitullo!'

Half the heads in the bus queue turned to stare. A girl of about Nicola's age, wearing school uniform, looked slowly and scornfully from Nicola to Rose and back again to Nicola. Nicola felt her cheeks turn an uncomfortable brick red. Why did Rose have to be so *awful*?

'What d'you mean?' she said, crossly. 'Rosemary Vitullo?'

'In the programme. It's what I'm going to be – my stage name.'

'What d'you want a stage name for?'

'Everybody has one.'

'No, they don't. Some people don't.'

'Only if they're called something nice to begin with . . . Mrs French used to be Pamela Weston, but her real name was Lake.'

'So what's wrong with that?'

'Pamela Lake in *Swan Lake*?'

'Why not?'

''Cos it sounds stupid.'

'So does Vitullo.'

'No, it doesn't.'

'Yes, it does, it sounds *stupid*. Anyway, I know where you got it from – you got it from that teacher at school. She'll probably sue you.'

'She can't, she's not there any more.'

27

'She could still sue you. There's probably a law against using other people's names.'

'Well, I'm not staying as Bruce. Bruce is horrible. It sounds like a dog.'

'I think it's wrong, changing your name,' said Nicola. 'I wouldn't change mine if I got famous.'

Rose spread out her arms to an imaginary audience.

'What could you ever be famous for?'

'Something.'

'What?'

'Haven't decided yet. Let's go and look in Beames's.'

Rose, momentarily diverted from her embarrassing antics, said, 'What's Beames's?'

'Shop that sells jokes – next door to the Co-op. Let's go and see if they've got any sneezing powder.'

Rose did a little hop.

'What d'you want sneezing powder for?'

'Makes you sneeze. Linda Baker had some at school, it's super. We were sneezing all the time in geography. Mr Drew thought it was an epidemic.'

'I bet he didn't really,' said Rose.

'Yes, he did. He said, it seems as though we've got the start of an epidemic – and then he told Linda she'd better not do PE if she was as bad as she sounded.'

'I wish I didn't have to do PE,' said Rose. 'I wish I could go to the Royal Ballet School and just do dancing.'

'You're only saying that because of Mrs French.'

'No, I'm not. I've *always* wanted to go there.'

'So why haven't you?'

''Cos you can't start till you're eleven, that's why.'

''Cos you never thought of it before, *that's* why... anyway, I don't expect you'd be good enough.'

Indignant spots of colour leapt into Rose's already pink cheeks.

'I bet I *would*!'

28

'I bet you wouldn't. You have to be *really* good to get into the Royal Ballet School. Linda Baker's got a cousin who's tried three times, and *she's* got gold medals.'

'So have I!' shrieked Rose. 'I've got gold medals!'

'Yours are only tap: *hers* were for ballet. You haven't got any for ballet.'

For one satisfying moment, Rose was silent; then sullenly she said, 'I bet I *could* get in, if I tried. I bet if I asked Mrs French she'd say I could.'

Nicola tossed her head.

'Ask her, then.'

'I will!'

'Bet she'll say you need gold medals.'

'Bet she won't! Bet she –'

'Oh, shut up,' said Nicola, suddenly growing bored. 'Let's go in and see if they've got any of this sneezing powder.'

The sneezing powder was available: it was the money which was not. Nicola, as usual, was broke. She always spent her pocket money within hours of receiving it. Rose, on the other hand, quite often saved hers. Nicola looked at her, hopefully.

'Why don't *you* buy some?'

'Don't want any,' said Rose.

'But it's only thirty p.'

Rose considered a while.

'I'll lend it you,' she said, at last. 'But you'll have to pay interest. People always pay interest. You'll have to pay –' she did some calculations on her fingers '– three p. And I want it back on Saturday otherwise it'll be *four* p.'

'All right,' said Nicola.

They walked up the road, with the packet of powder. Nicola took a quick look inside, just to make sure that it was the same sort as Linda Baker had had: Rose peered disparagingly over her shoulder.

'Is that all it is? Looks like curry powder to me . . . I bet that's what it is. I bet it's curry powder.'

"Tisn't!' Nicola snatched the bag away, jealously. 'It's special stuff that makes you sneeze.'

'Bet it wouldn't make me sneeze.'

'Course it would! They couldn't sell it if it didn't work. Here –' She pushed the bag back again. 'Try it and see.'

Cautiously, Rose dipped her nose inside. In fairness, it was quite a small nose. It wasn't really the big, red, beaky thing that Nicola liked to sing about.

'There you are!' Rose raised her head, triumphant: not even the suspicion of a sneeze. 'Told you it wouldn't do anything.'

'That's because you didn't get enough. You have to *sniff* at it, not just hover over it.'

Rose puckered her lips uncertainly.

'Miss Joyce says it's not good for you, sniffing things.'

'That's glue, stupid! She didn't mean sneezing powder . . . go on! Do it properly.'

Still, Rose hesitated.

'I don't like the smell of it.'

'You won't *notice* the smell once you're sneezing – anyway, you've got to, now. It wouldn't be fair if you didn't.'

'Oh, all *right*.'

None too happily, Rose plunged her nose back into the bag. Nicola waited, in expectation. Quite suddenly, Rose gave a scream. The bag fell to the ground as both hands flew up to her face.

'What's the matter? What's the matter?'

Nicola stared at her sister in alarm. The forget-me-not eyes had gone all big and swimmy. Tears were coursing down her cheeks, mingling with the traces of powder to form great yellow-brown stains. Nothing like this had happened at school. What they'd done at school, they'd all sprinkled a bit on the backs of their hands and sniffed at it just before going into class. They'd started sneezing almost immediately – Mr Drew really *had* thought there was an epidemic. Everyone had sneezed and sneezed. Rose wasn't sneezing so much as wheezing – as well as she could, for sobbing.

'What *is* it?' said Nicola. People were beginning to stare. Trust Rose to make a scene. 'What's the *matter*?'

'It hurts! It hurts!'

Rose roared the words at a hundred decibels. Heads turned, in all directions, and a lady who had stopped to watch now came over and said briskly, 'Where does it hurt? Can you breathe properly?' which Nicola couldn't help thinking was rather a silly question, seeing as Rose was yelling at the top of her voice. Rose, however, who always responded to an audience, only sobbed the louder and dramatically declared that she could hardly breathe at *all*.

'But where does it hurt? Not your chest?'

'Everywhere!' shrieked Rose. 'It hurts the back of my nose and it hurts my eyes and it hurts my throat and –'

The lady turned sternly to Nicola.

'Where does she live? Do you know?'

Nicola swallowed, and pointed down the High Street.

'Just over there. Fenning Road.'

'Then we'd better take her home straight away. Come along, little one! Let's get you back to Mummy.'

Nicola felt slightly sick – partly at Rose being addressed as little one, and partly at the thought of what Mrs Bruce was likely to say when she saw the state she was in.

Mrs Bruce said exactly what Nicola had feared she would say, 'For goodness' *sake*, Nicola! What have you done *now*?' Unfortunately, that was not all that she said. When Rose had been pacified and tucked into her bed with an aspirin and a mug of hot chocolate, and when the doctor had been telephoned and had made reassuring noises about no harm being likely to have been done, and agreeing noises about it being criminal that shops should sell such things, and certainly it ought to be looked into, she said a great deal more.

'I don't blame you for buying the stuff – I blame the shop for selling it. What I *do* blame you for is bullying Rose into sniffing at it.'

'I didn't,' said Nicola. 'I didn't bully her.'

'She says that you did. She says she didn't want to sniff it, but that you made her.'

'I didn't *make* her. She wanted to know if it worked.'

'Well, now you've discovered that it doesn't, so perhaps you'll be satisfied. Another time, just think before you do these things. It could have been disastrous. Surely to goodness you're old enough to know that you don't go about sniffing substances that could be dangerous?'

'I didn't know it was dangerous! A girl at school had some. We –'

'Oh, so it's going round the school, is it?' Mrs Bruce pursed her lips. 'In that case, I think I'd better come up and have a word with Mr Henry before someone really gets themselves hurt.'

'It's only *sneezing* powder.' Nicola was growing desperate. Her mother coming to see Mr Henry was the last thing she wanted. Linda Baker would be furious. 'It doesn't *do* anything.'

'What do you mean, it doesn't do anything? You saw what it did to Rose.'

Nicola felt like saying, 'Oh, well, *Rose*.' It would do something, to Rose. Everyone knew that Rose enjoyed being the centre of attention. She only had to fall over in the playground to stand there blubbering until a member of staff came running up and made a fuss of her.

'It could have been extremely nasty.' Mrs Bruce sounded cross. She obviously didn't think Nicola was showing sufficient repentance. 'It could have affected her breathing – she might even have had to go to hospital. Then how would you have felt?'

Nicola looked down at the floor and didn't say anything.

'You wouldn't have felt very good, would you? No. Well, then . . . you just think about it. As it is, we've been lucky. The doctor thinks she'll probably have nothing more than a sore throat and a bit of a headache, though goodness knows that's bad enough. She won't be able to go to rehearsal tonight, that's one thing you've achieved. Mrs French isn't going to be very happy with you.'

I bet *I*'d go to rehearsal, thought Nicola. I bet I wouldn't let a sore throat stop me. I bet I'd go if I was *dying*.

'You'd better run down the road,' said Mrs Bruce, 'and explain to her what's happened. Tell her that you're very sorry, but your sister won't be able to be there – and you can tell her why, while you're about it.'

'What, me?' Nicola was resentful. It wasn't her fault Rose was lying in bed pretending to be ill. *She* hadn't told her to sniff half the bag up her nose. Anyone with any sense would have known. 'Why should I have to go and do it?' It was bad enough, knowing that Rose had pinched her part – *her* part, that *she* had been wanted for – without having to go and make excuses for why she couldn't turn up. 'Why can't you telephone?'

'Because I don't wish to telephone! I wish you to go round there and explain, as politely as you can, what has happened. I should think in the circumstances it's the very *least* you can do. You can eat your tea, then you can get straight round there – and mind you give her the full version. Just remember . . . I shall be checking!'

4

The house that Mrs French lived in was old and tall, with a broad flight of steps leading up to the front door and others that went down to a basement. Nicola wasn't sure whether she ought to go upwards or downwards. She had a vague idea that basements were strictly for delivery boys and servants (in the days when there had been such things) but the front door seemed far too grand for common-or-garden mortals such as herself to use. She wondered what Rose would do, if Rose were here – and knew at once that Rose, without the least hesitation in the world, would go marching up to the front door. All right, then: if Rose could do it, so could she.

Determinedly, she climbed the steps, taking them sedately one at a time instead of at her usual full-tilted gallop. The front door had two stained glass panels and a big black knocker in the shape of a lion's head, the actual knocking part being an iron ring which the lion held clamped between his teeth. Look as hard as she might she couldn't find any signs of a bell, so gingerly, scared of setting up too much of a racket (Mrs Bruce was forever complaining of the noise she made) she took hold of the iron ring and let it fall back against the door. It didn't seem to make much of a sound, but obviously somebody must have heard it, for a light had been turned on in the hall and was shining through the stained glass panels. The door opened and there was Mrs French, dressed in a sweater and jeans, with her hair in a pony tail. She looked surprised to see Nicola.

'Hallo, Nicola! Did you knock?'

'Yes,' said Nicola.

'Really? I didn't hear it – you'll have to learn to be a bit bolder! I only came down because I thought I heard the gate go. So, what can I do for you?'

'My mother said I was to come and say that I'm very sorry but Rose won't be able to be at the rehearsal tonight.'

'Oh, dear! That's a blow. I hope she's not poorly?'

'She took sneezing powder,' said Nicola, 'and made herself ill.'

'Took sneezing powder? Good gracious! That doesn't sound a very Rose thing to do. Is she going to be all right?'

'She's just got a bit of a headache and a sore throat. And actually –' she had to force herself to say it '– actually, it was my fault. She said I was to tell you. She said she was going to check.'

'Did she, indeed?' Mrs French pulled a face. 'Then I must remember that you've faithfully carried out instructions . . . in what way was it your fault?'

Nicola hesitated. She didn't really believe that it *had* been her fault. Not altogether.

'I suppose,' she said, grudgingly, 'because it was my sneezing powder.'

'Ah!' Mrs French laughed. 'That sounds more like it . . . I couldn't imagine *Rose!*'

'She didn't have to sniff it,' said Nicola.

'No, I'm sure she didn't. But since she did, and since it *was* your sneezing powder, I really think you ought to pay penance, don't you?'

Nicola frowned, not quite certain what penance meant. If it meant handing over money, then she couldn't, because she hadn't got any. Specially not now that she owed Rose thirty p. – thirty-*three* p. – and all for nothing. That was the really bitterest part of it. A whole packet of perfectly good sneezing powder just left there, lying on the pavement, for nine and a half million feet to trample on. It'd probably be ground into dust by now. Why the silly cow couldn't have held on to it –

'How about taking her place?' said Mrs French. 'At the rehearsal? We really do need someone there, even if it's only to get the timing right . . . how about it? Just for this evening? I'm sure you could do it.'

Nicola was sure she could, too. She didn't know whether to scowl and mumble, or stand on her head by way of jubilation. In the end, she didn't do either, but simply pushed her fringe out of her eyes with one finger and said carelessly, 'All right. I don't mind.'

'Good! I'll pick you up in about –' Mrs French looked at her watch '– about quarter of an hour. Tell your mother I'll bring you back again, of course, as I do Rose.'

'All right,' said Nicola.

As she reached the bottom of the steps, Mrs French called after her, 'You don't by any chance have a pair of ballet shoes, do you? No? Well, not to worry . . . bring some plimsolls. They'll do just as well.'

Mrs Bruce didn't believe it when Nicola said that she was to take Rose's place at the rehearsal.

'You? What's she want you for?'

'She says she needs someone to be there even if it's only to get the timing right.'

'Well, she won't get it right with you around, that's for sure!'

'Why won't she?' said Nicola.

'Because you don't know anything about it . . . what do you know about counting bars?'

Nothing; she didn't know anything. She didn't even know for certain what a bar was. Rose was the one that was musical. Rose always had been, right from her cradle. She *hated* Rose. Sullenly, she said, 'I might as well not go, then.'

37

'Oh, you'll have to go if you've said you will. Just try to behave yourself and do what you're asked to do. It's only the one night. Rose will be back again on Sunday.'

The rehearsal took place in a room attached to one of the local churches (the one with the gargoyles). It had big coloured pictures of Jesus hanging on the walls, which just at first Nicola found rather off-putting. It didn't seem right to be pulling faces and sticking out her tongue in front of Jesus – it seemed almost as bad as if she were doing it in front of Mr Henry, at school. But then, after a while, she became so absorbed in the story that she didn't really care. She forgot about Jesus, and concentrated all her attention on being a bad little girl – *the* Bad Little Girl. The part that by rights should have been hers. She was sure Rose couldn't do it properly. Rose simply didn't know anything about being bad.

To her great relief, she found that there wasn't any question of counting bars. The music – played on an old upright piano that stood in a corner by a fat lady wearing hundreds of cardigans – was the busy, bouncing sort where you knew automatically when you had to come in and when you had to do things.

She was rather surprised to find that it wasn't Mrs French who was in charge of the rehearsal, but a small, bandy man called Mr Marlowe. Mrs French was playing the part of the Elder Sister. There was Mama and Papa, Elder Sister, Elder Brother, Nursemaid with Baby (Baby was only a doll), Bad Little Girl, Good Little Boy and Photographer. Mr Marlowe played the Photographer as well as conducting the rehearsal. Nicola thought it was hilarious. He was pretending to use an old-fashioned camera, which meant that he had to keep pulling an imaginary cover over his head whenever he looked through the lens. Every time he stopped being the Photographer in order to go back to being the man in charge of rehearsal, he would solemnly pause to remove the non-existent cover from his head before addressing them. The lady playing Mama, seeing Nicola convulsed with giggles, explained that it wasn't quite as silly as it might seem.

'One of the secrets of being a successful mime is really to *feel* the object that you're miming; so that if you were miming a jug of milk, say, and the front door bell suddenly rang, you wouldn't just let go of it in mid-air, you'd put it down on a table. That's why Ted has to keep taking his cover off . . . he really does *feel* that he's got his head underneath it, and obviously, if he has, then he can't speak properly, can he? We wouldn't be able to hear him.'

Nicola was much struck by this view of things. She tried very hard to remember it when her turn came. Mr Marlowe had explained to her that what she had to do was take an imaginary mouse out of the pocket of her imaginary dress (Mrs French had already told her what sort of dress it would be, and where the pocket was to be found) and she was to hold it up to the camera so that it could have its picture taken. At a certain point in the music – the bit where the piano did a sudden twiddle and went PLONK – the mouse was going to escape, on-purpose-by-accident, into the room. Nicola and everybody else had to follow it with their eyes, so that the audience would know where it was and what it was doing. (What it did in the end was run up Elder Sister's dress, so that Elder Sister screamed and jumped on her chair.)

'Remember, Nicola,' said Mr Marlowe, 'we really have to *see* that it's a mouse. Not a doll, or a ball, or anything like that. It's got to be a mouse, or people won't understand what's going on.'

Nicola didn't have any trouble at all imagining a mouse. She had had a mouse of her own once upon a time. Unfortunately, she had forgotten to shut his cage properly one day and he had got out and frightened Rose into hysterics, so that Mrs Bruce had said that if she wasn't going to look after him properly he would have to go, but she could still remember the way he had felt in her hands, all warm and tiny and quick-moving. She wondered why Rose hadn't mentioned anything about this particular bit. She'd mentioned almost everything else. It was odd, thought Nicola, considering this was one of the most important bits there was. After all, if the mouse didn't escape then the Elder Sister wouldn't scream and jump on her chair, and Papa wouldn't hold the Bad Little Girl up by one ear and shake her, and the Elder Brother and the Photographer wouldn't go running round the room brandishing fire irons; and if nobody did any of that, then half the fun would be gone.

Nicola concentrated very hard, therefore, on making her mouse into a real mouse – so much so that when Mr Marlowe, emerging from his cover, suddenly cried, 'Cut! Polly, darling, could you move a bit further in? That's better . . . all right, let's take it again,' she was very careful to restore him to her imaginary pocket before folding her hands once more in her lap and resuming her pose. She knew that the mouse was real for *her*, because when he finally escaped she could actually see him scurrying across the floor, so that it was all she could do not to go chasing after him. Whether or not she had made him real for other people she wasn't sure, but she thought perhaps she must have done because at the end, when the photograph had at last been taken and the scene was over, Mr Marlowe called out, 'Splendid mouse, Nicola! Well done! What colour was it?'

Nicola answered without hesitation, 'White, with brown ears,' because that was what her own mouse had been; and everybody laughed except Mr Marlowe, who said, 'No, seriously, it's important . . . if she hadn't known what colour it was, I'd have been extremely disappointed. OK, everyone! Let's have a quick coffee, then run it once more.'

The lady with the cardigans, whom everyone called

Marge, was already busy with a kettle and an array of mugs which stood on a table near the piano. For Nicola and the Good Little Boy (his name was Mark and he was six years old and looked almost too good to be true) there was a choice between hot milk and lemonade. Nicola had lemonade, because she thought that Rose would probably have had hot milk. Mark also had lemonade, because he said he'd had hot milk once and there'd been a skin on it.

'Ugh!' said Nicola. 'Horrid!'

'Rose always drinks hers,' said Mark.

'Rose *would*.'

Mark looked at her, solemnly. He had huge grey eyes in a small, heart-shaped face topped by a cap of thick gold hair. Nicola could quite understand why it was that he had had to be a *good* little boy. He was even more unsuited to badness than Rose.

'Isn't Rose coming back any more?' he said.

'Don't know.' She did know, of course. To say that she didn't simply wasn't true. Still, she'd said it now.

'I wouldn't mind,' said Mark, 'if she didn't. I'd sooner have you. I like your mouse better than I like hers.'

'*Do* you?' said Nicola.

'Yes, I do,' said Mark; and he nodded, to emphasize the fact. 'I think it was a super mouse. I could see that it was brown and white.'

'Brown ears,' said Nicola.

'Brown ears,' said Mark. 'I could see it.'

Nicola beamed. Really, she thought, in spite of looking so terribly good, Mark was quite a nice little boy. That was something else that Rose had never mentioned.

Mrs French, who had taken her coffee away into a corner with Mr Marlowe, suddenly turned and beckoned to her. She had a smile on her face, so Nicola knew it couldn't be that she'd done anything wrong. She bounced across, still beaming.

'Nicola –' Mrs French held out a hand. 'We wanted to ask

you something . . . how would you feel about playing the part of the Bad Little Girl all the time?'

Nicola's beam turned into a half-witted gape.

'Instead of Rose?'

'It's the mouse, you see.' Mr Marlowe sounded apologetic. 'We've never been too sure that your sister actually likes mice.'

'No, she doesn't,' said Nicola. 'She goes into hysterics.'

'Ah! That would account for it.'

Account for what? wondered Nicola. Had Rose been going into hysterics at rehearsals?

'Tell me,' said Mrs French. She leaned forward, on her chair. 'Would Rose be very upset, do you think, if you did the part instead of her?'

Nicola thought about it.

'Yes,' she said. 'I expect so.'

Mrs French and Mr Marlowe exchanged glances.

'Suppose we wrote Rose in as something else?' That was Mr Marlowe. 'We could always use another sister.'

'A good little sister to go with the good little brother?'

'Why not? They could come in together, holding hands.'

'And what would she do while the mouse chase was going on?'

'Well –' Mr Marlowe made a gesture. 'She could always run across to Nurse and hide in her petticoats.'

'Mm . . . yes. That's not a bad idea. It wouldn't be such a good part as the one she's got now, of course.'

'No, but it would still be a part. It would be up to her what she made of it.'

'True.' Mrs French turned back to Nicola. 'How do you feel about it, Nicola? Would you like to play the Bad Little Girl?'

Would she? She'd been playing it in secret for weeks. Mr Marlowe laughed.

'I can see by her face that she would . . . all right, then, Supermouse! The part's yours.'

'But don't forget,' said Mrs French, quickly. 'We want Rose as Youngest Sister. You'll tell her that, won't you?'

Nicola nodded, breathlessly. She was too delirious for speech.

'We mustn't make it sound as if we don't want her any more. It wouldn't be fair just to discard her. She's put in a lot of hard work, after all.'

'Oh, yes,' said Mr Marlowe. 'She's a proper little trouper. No denying that.'

'Just not right for this particular part.'

'Unlike old Supermouse here.' Mr Marlowe grinned: Nicola grinned back. 'Come on, then, Supermouse!' He set his coffee cup to one side. 'Let's be having you . . . time we got stuck in again.'

It was half-past nine when Mrs French dropped Nicola off in Fenning Road.

'Don't forget,' she said. 'Tell Rose we definitely still want her.'

'Yes. All right.' Nicola, in her eagerness, was already through the gate and half way up the path. 'I'll tell her.'

She hopped up the step into the front porch and jabbed her finger on the bell, keeping it pressed there till someone should come.

'What's all the panic?' It was her father who eventually opened the door. 'Don't tell me they've landed at last?'

'Who?' Nicola paused, impatiently, already poised for flight.

'The little green men,' said Mr Bruce.

'Oh!' She didn't have time, just now, for her father's jokes; she had news to break. She tore across the hall and into the sitting room. 'Mrs French wants me to –'

The words died on her lips: Rose was there, curled up in pyjamas and dressing gown on the sofa. She had obviously been allowed to come downstairs and watch television to make up for having missed the rehearsal.

'Mrs French wants you to what?'

Her mother twisted round to look at her. Nicola stood awkwardly on one leg in the doorway. Somehow, with Rose there, all triumph had gone.

'She wants me to –'

'Well?'

'She wants me to do the part –'

She tried not to look at Rose as she said it, but her eyes *would* go sliding over, just for a quick glance. A quick glance was enough: Rose's pink cheeks had turned bright scarlet, her freckles standing out like splotches of brown paint carelessly flicked off the end of a paint brush. Nicola forced herself to look at something else. It seemed too much like spying, to look at Rose.

Mr Bruce came back in, closing the door behind him. He gave Nicola a little push.

'Born in a field?'

Nicola didn't say anything. He was always saying 'Born in a field?' when she didn't close doors behind her. Mrs Bruce, leaning forward to see round her husband as he crossed back to his arm chair, said, 'What do you mean, she wants you to do the part?'

'She wants me to do it – instead of Rose. But it's all right,' said Nicola. 'She still wants Rose. She wants Rose to play another part . . . she wants her to be the *good* little sister.'

'There isn't any good little sister!' Rose's voice was all high and strangulated. 'There isn't any such part!'

'They're going to write it in,' said Nicola, 'specially for you. Mr Marlowe said you were a proper little trouper, and Mrs French said you'd done a lot of hard work and it wouldn't be fair to – to discard you. So they're going to make this other part, and you're going to come in with the Good Little Boy, and hold his hand, and –'

'I don't want to hold his hand! I don't want another part!' Tears came spurting out of Rose's eyes. 'I want my own part!'

44

'Hush, now, Rose, there's obviously been some r
Did you tell Mrs French, as I told you –' her mothe
at Nicola, mistrustfully '– that the reason Rose couldn't
come to rehearsal this evening was because you'd made her
sniff powder up her nose?'

Nicola nodded.

'*Did* you?'

'Yes! I did! That's why she made me take her place. She
said I'd got to pay pence.'

'Pay pence?' Mrs Bruce looked bewildered. 'What are you
talking about?'

'What she said . . . she said I'd got to pay pence.'

'Penance,' said Mr Bruce. 'Do I take it we have some sort
of crisis on our hands?'

Mrs Bruce tightened her lips.

'Nothing we can't get sorted out. Rose, do for heaven's
sake stop making that noise! How can I get to the bottom of
things if I can't hear myself speak?'

Rose subsided, snuffling, into her dressing gown. Mr
Bruce, shaking his head, disappeared into his paper. He
usually washed his hands of it when it came to what he
called 'female squabbles'.

'Now, then!' Mrs Bruce turned back again to Nicola. Her
voice was brisk and businesslike. It was the voice she used
when she suspected someone of not telling her the entire
truth. It meant, *let us get down to brass tacks and have no more of
this nonsense*. 'What exactly did Mrs French say?'

'She said, how would I feel like playing the part of the Bad
Little Girl all the time.'

'Instead of Rose?'

'It's because of the mouse. Rose can't do the mouse the
same as I can.'

'Yes, I can!' Rose sat bolt upright on the sofa.

'No, you can't,' said Nicola. 'You don't like mice.'

'What's that matter? It's not a *real* mouse.'

45

'But you have to pretend that it is! You have to *feel* it –'

'I do feel it! I feel it all wriggling and horrible!'

'If you thought it was horrible,' said Nicola, 'you wouldn't have it with you in the first place.'

'Yes, I would!'

'No, you –'

'Do they have to?' said Mr Bruce.

'No, they don't.' Mrs Bruce spoke scoldingly. 'Be quiet, the pair of you! This is ridiculous. How can Nicola possibly take over the part at this late stage? Rose has been rehearsing it for weeks.'

'Anyway, what's *she* know about it?' Rose jerked her head, pettishly, in Nicola's direction. '*She's* never acted.'

'Quite. I really think, Nicola, you're being just a tiny bit selfish. When it's Rose who's done all the hard preliminary work . . . just to come waltzing in and reap the benefit. It's not very sisterly, is it?'

Nicola stuck out her lower lip. Her mother, seeing it, changed tack. Her voice became coaxing.

'You know how much it means to Rose. For you, it's just fun. For Rose – well! For Rose it's everything. After all, she's the one who's going to make it her career. It really means something to Rose. Surely –'

She broke off and smiled, hopefully. Nicola said nothing. She could be stubborn, when she wanted; and now that she'd got the part, she certainly wasn't going to be talked into giving it up just to satisfy Rose.

'Make her!' Rose's voice rang out, shrill and accusing from the sofa. 'Make her say she won't do it!'

'I can't make her,' said Mrs Bruce. 'It must be Nicola's own decision.'

Her father lowered his paper and looked at Nicola over the top of it.

'I suppose you couldn't just say yes and keep them happy?'

Why should I? thought Nicola.

'After all . . . anything for a quiet life.' Mr Bruce winked at her. He quite often winked at Nicola over the heads of Rose and her mother. It was supposed to convey a sense of fellow feeling: Us Lads against Them Womenfolk. Usually she responded, but today she did not. She just went on standing there, stony-faced, in silence.

'No?' said Mr Bruce. 'In that case –' he raised his paper again '– there's nothing more to be said. She's been offered the part, she obviously wants to do it, so let's not have any argument. Rose will just have to take a back seat for once.'

Mrs Bruce looked at her husband, frowningly.

'It really isn't playing fair, to take away a part that's already been given to someone else . . . I'm surprised that Mrs French would do such a thing.'

'But I was the one she wanted all along!'

The words had slipped out before she could stop them. Mrs Bruce turned, sharply.

'How do you know?'

'Because – because she told me.'

'She didn't!' screamed Rose. 'It's a lie!'

''Tisn't a lie!'

'It is! It is! Why should anyone want you? You can't dance! You can't –'

'Rose, be quiet! *And* you, Nicola. Brawling like a couple of alley cats. You can both get up to bed.'

It was rare for Mrs Bruce to grow as cross with Rose as she did with Nicola. Rose pouted, but none the less humped herself off the sofa. She trailed rebelliously in Nicola's wake to the door.

'Good,' said Mr Bruce. He rustled his newspaper. 'If that's all settled –'

'It's not all settled.' Mrs Bruce plumped up the cushion where Rose had been sitting. 'As soon as you two get back from school tomorrow we're going down the road to talk to

47

Mrs French. We'll see what *she* has to say about it. In the meantime, you can both of you get upstairs and put yourselves to bed ... I've had quite enough of your bickering for one evening.'

5

The next day, after tea, both Rose and Nicola were marched
down the road to Mrs French. They stood on the front steps
behind their mother as she knocked at the door with the
lion's head knocker.

'Now you'll see,' said Rose.

They were the first words she had addressed to Nicola all
day. Nicola didn't deign to reply. She was thinking, if Mrs
French lets her have the part back, it will be the meanest
thing I ever heard . . .

It was Mr French who opened the door – at least, Nicola
assumed that it was Mr French. He was youngish, and good-
looking, with long, curly black hair and a gold chain round
his neck with a medallion hanging from it. When Mrs Bruce
explained that they had come to see Mrs French, he twisted
round to look at a grandfather clock in the hall and said,
'Can you bear to wait five minutes? She won't be long, she's
just giving a class. Due to finish any time now.'

He led them through into a front room which was
cluttered with books and stacks of gramophone records.

'Sorry about the mess – we've never quite got around to
finding a home for everything. We're still having the place
done up, which means only half the rooms are habitable.
Now, what can I offer you? Can I offer you a coffee? No?
You're sure? Well, in that case perhaps you'll excuse me if I
slope off. She shouldn't be too long.'

As Mr French left the room, Rose turned excitedly to her
mother.

'I didn't know Mrs French gave *classes*.'

'I expect they need the money. Big place like this . . . must cost a lot to keep up.'

Rose clearly wasn't interested in what things cost to keep up: her mind was running on quite other lines.

'Do you think *I* could have classes with her?'

'You?' Mrs Bruce looked at her in surprise. 'Why should you want classes with her? What's wrong with Madam Paula?'

'Nothing,' said Rose. 'But Mrs *French* used to be with the Royal Ballet.'

'That doesn't necessarily make her a good teacher. In any case, you don't want to specialize in ballet. You've always said you want to be in musicals.'

'She's changed her mind,' said Nicola. 'She wants to go to the Royal Ballet School now.'

'*Do* you?'

Rose had turned pink beneath her freckles. She shot Nicola a venomous glare.

'I've always wanted to.'

'I never knew that! Why on earth didn't you say so before?'

''Cos she never thought of it before.'

'Yes, I did! I thought of it –'

'Enough!' Mrs Bruce held up a hand. 'Don't for heaven's sake start that again.'

'But I did think of it before! I thought of it *ages* ago.'

'Then you should have said ages ago. We could have done something about it.'

'We still could,' said Rose. 'You don't start there till you're eleven. If I could have classes with Mrs French – *can* I have classes with Mrs French?'

'But what about Madam Paula? She mightn't like it.'

'It wouldn't matter about Madam Paula if I was going to the Royal Ballet School . . . *can* I? *Please*? Say that I can!'

'Well . . . I don't know. I suppose, if you're really set on it –'

'I *am*,' said Rose. '*Honestly*. I really *am*. I've been set on it for *years*. I've –'

'All right, all right! You've made your point. I believe you.'

'So will you ask her? This evening? *Will* you?'

'Yes, yes, I'll ask her this evening . . . as your father would say, anything for a quiet life.'

Rose beamed, triumphantly, in Nicola's direction: she'd got her own way again. She was *always* getting her own way.

Mrs French came in wearing black tights and a sweater, with her hair pulled back into a knot, the way it had been that first day, on the building site.

'Hallo, Mrs Bruce! Rose, Nicola . . . what's all this?' She laughed. 'A deputation?'

Nicola, embarrassed, sat on her hands on the extreme edge of a leather arm chair, whilst Rose moved up closer to her mother on the sofa.

'I hope it's not inconveniencing you.'

Mrs Bruce made it sound as though even if it were she had no intention of going away again. Nicola cringed. If the leather arm chair had had a cushion she would have put it on her head and pretended not to be there. As it hadn't, she kept her eyes fixed firmly on a pile of books which had been stacked in the hearth. The top one was called *Theatre Street* by somebody whose name she couldn't pronounce: Tamara Kar-sav-in-a (Karsa-vina?) She heard Mrs French say, 'No, not at all! As a matter of fact, I'd just come to the end of a class, so you chose a good moment – that's a very famous book, by the way, Nicola. Written by a famous Russian ballerina. You can borrow it, if you like.'

'Can I?' Nicola looked up, avidly. She liked it when people offered to lend you their books: it showed they trusted you.

'Remind me to let you have it before you leave.' Mrs French perched herself amiably on the arm of another leather chair, similar to the one that Nicola was sitting in. 'You might like to read it as well, Rose. It's all about life in a Russian ballet school.'

Rose looked dubious: she wasn't much of a reader. She tugged, impatiently, at her mother's arm. Mrs Bruce, who had been starting to say something, broke off.

'What?' She bent her head. Rose whispered, urgently. 'Oh, yes! All right. Let's get that out of the way first . . . Rose is nagging me to know whether it would be possible for her to take some classes with you. Apparently, she's set her heart on going to the Royal Ballet School –'

'The Royal *Ballet* School?'

The way Mrs French said it, Nicola was pleased to note, she made it sound as if Rose were asking to have tea with the Queen. She couldn't have made it clearer that in her opinion Rose didn't stand a chance. A warm glow of satisfaction slowly spread itself through Nicola's body. So much for Rose. Maybe she *wasn't* so wonderful, after all.

'It's an extremely difficult place to get in to, you know.'

'I know,' said Rose. She sounded complacent: if anyone could get in there, *she* should be able to.

'Did you know that out of every four hundred applicants only about thirty are chosen? And at least ten of those will be boys?'

Rose made a little pouting motion with her lips.

'She has been dancing a long time,' said Mrs Bruce. 'Ever since she was four years old. She's had a lot of experience.'

'Ah, but it's not just a question of experience, Mrs Bruce –'

'You need gold medals.' Nicola couldn't help it: she *had* to say it. 'You need gold medals, don't you?'

'Well, no, as a matter of fact, you don't! You not only don't need gold medals, you don't even need to have done a step of ballet in your life. In fact, sometimes they prefer it if people haven't, because it means they won't have been able to develop any bad habits.'

'I'm sure Rose hasn't developed any bad habits,' said Mrs Bruce.

'Well, no, it's quite possible that she hasn't. I'm just pointing out that a totally inexperienced girl stands every bit as much chance of getting in as one who's been doing it since she was a baby . . . Nicola, for example.' Mrs French paused. 'She'd stand just as much chance as Rose.'

Rose didn't like that. Nicola could see that she didn't. Mrs Bruce, quite plainly, didn't believe it.

'Surely,' she said, 'there has to be natural talent?'

'Oh, yes! Yes, that's the very thing they're looking for – that plus the right physique. Lots of girls are turned down simply because they don't meet the physical requirements. It doesn't mean they can't still go on to be dancers. There's no reason on earth why Rose shouldn't have a go, if she wants. I'm just warning her not to be disappointed, that's all.'

'Perhaps if she were to take a few classes with you first –'

'I'm afraid that wouldn't be possible, Mrs Bruce. You see, I don't teach full time – I only take a very few selected pupils. Usually girls who are already in the profession. I very very rarely work with the younger ones. Only in the most exceptional cases.'

Mrs Bruce bristled slightly: she was accustomed to think of Rose as being exceptional.

'You know what I feel?' said Mrs French. 'I feel that Rose is far too much of an all-round performer to tie herself down to just one branch of show business. Especially ballet, which is so restricting. Where does she have classes at the moment?'

'She goes to Madam Paula's. It's where she's always gone.'

'Then I think that's exactly where she ought to keep on going. It'll not only give her a good general grounding as a dancer, it'll provide her with the opportunity to develop any other talents she may have, as well. Who knows? She might have potential as an actress, or a singer –'

'Oh, she has.' Mrs Bruce nodded. 'Madam Paula's already told us. In fact, she's going up to London for an audition later this month. It's for *Little Women – The March Girls*, they're calling it. We're hoping she might stand a chance as Amy.'

'I'm sure she'd make a lovely Amy.' Mrs French smiled. Rose smiled back, uncertainly. Nicola could tell that she was trying to make up her mind whether the thought of making a lovely Amy was sufficient compensation for not being considered exceptional enough to have classes with Mrs French.

'Even if she doesn't get one of the leads,' said Mrs Bruce, 'I keep telling her, there's bound to be lots of other parts.'

'Well, of course.'

'I always think it's worth trying. It'll stand her in good stead later, when she's doing it for real.'

'Yes, indeed. I'm all for people having a go.'

There was a silence. Nicola looked down again at the pile of books. She didn't know why, but she had the feeling Mrs French wasn't really very interested in Rose. It was odd, because people usually were. You'd have thought, being a dancer, that Mrs French would be.

'Anyway –' Mrs Bruce cleared her throat. 'The thing we really came about was this part that Rose is doing for you. Nicola said something about you wanting her to take over. I told her, it's ridiculous, at this late stage. She must have got it wrong.'

'She hasn't got it wrong, Mrs Bruce. I did ask her if she'd like to, but only because we have something else in mind for Rose – we do quite definitely still want Rose. Did Nicola not tell you?'

'Yes!' Nicola's head jerked up, indignantly. 'I did tell her! I told her you wanted Rose for the youngest sister.'

'That's right.' Mrs French nodded. 'We decided that what we'd like was a Good Little Girl to go with the Good Little Boy – Rose struck us as being the very person. As you say, it is rather late to be changing things round, but Nicola already seemed to know most of the Bad Little Girl's part, and I have every confidence in Rose being able to pick things up just as quickly as if she were a pro – which, indeed, she practically is! Certainly she will be if she gets into the West End.'

Mrs Bruce looked round, doubtfully, at Rose.

'The only thing is, she seems to think it's not a proper part.'

'Oh, but it is! I assure you . . we're writing it in specially.'

Rose, burying her head in her mother's shoulder, made some utterance that only Mrs Bruce could hear. Mrs Bruce patted her hand, consolingly.

'I'm sure Mrs French will do what she can. You must remember, though . . . it's not always the largest parts that are the best parts. Not by any manner of means. Isn't that so?' She appealed to Mrs French, who said, 'Any professional will tell you, Rose . . . a part's what you make it.'

'Not if it's not a real one.' The words came out, muffled, from Rose's buried head. 'Not if it's just a *pretend* one.'

'But it's not a pretend one! Mrs French has already told you . . . she's writing it in specially.'

'I don't want it! I want the other one – the one I had before!'

Mrs Bruce looked up; half apologetic, half accusing.

'It is very upsetting for a child, to have something that's been given her suddenly taken away.'

'Yes, I do realize that, Mrs Bruce. That's why I've made sure she's being offered something else.'

'I don't want something else!'

'Not even if it's something that's far better suited to you? Just think! No more horrible mice!'

'She's worked very hard at that mouse,' said Mrs Bruce.

'Yes.' Mrs French sighed. 'We really do appreciate all the work she's put in. That's why we don't want to lose her. But you do know, don't you, Rose –' leaving her perch on the arm of the leather chair, Mrs French sank down, gracefully, on to her heels beside the still sniffling Rose '– you do know that if you're going to go into the profession you'll have to be prepared to take some pretty hard knocks? It won't do you any good just sitting down and crying – you have to learn to take the rough with the smooth. Things don't always work out just the way we'd like them to. Suppose, for instance, you were offered the part of Amy, and then suddenly the director decided that the girl playing Beth would be better as Amy, and that you'd be better as Beth –'

'I wouldn't mind playing Beth! Beth's a *real* part.'

'But so is the Youngest Sister . . . I promise you! You'll have plenty of things to do.'

'I don't want to play the Youngest Sister! I want to be the Bad Little Girl!'

Mrs French sat back on her heels. Mrs Bruce looked at her, challengingly, as if to say, 'Well? And what now?' Rose just sat there, weeping. Nicola regarded her sister with contempt. All this fuss over a mere *part*.

'Dear oh dear!' Mrs French shook her head. 'The last thing I wanted to do was cause any unhappiness. I'd hoped I'd managed to find a satisfactory solution . . . now what do we do? I can't very well ask Nicola to play the Youngest Sister, can I?'

There was a silence, broken only by Rose's snuffles. Nicola could guess what she was thinking. She was thinking that as far as she was concerned there wasn't any reason why Nicola should be asked to play anything at all. Mrs Bruce was probably thinking exactly the same thing.

'I suppose –' Mrs French spoke pleadingly to Rose '– I suppose you couldn't possibly think of the production as a whole? How much better it would be if we had a really *bad* Bad Little Girl and a really *good* Good Little Sister?'

Rose buttoned her lips.

'No.' Mrs French pulled a rueful face. 'I suppose not. I should have stuck to my guns right at the beginning – it's my own fault. I just didn't want to cause any ructions in the family. Now it looks as though I've caused one anyway.' With an air of somewhat weary resignation, she rose to her feet. 'I honestly don't know what to say, Mrs Bruce. I've offered Rose another part; what more can I do? I can only repeat that we should be extremely sorry to lose her – and that the part *is* a real part, if she cares to make it one. It's entirely up to her. If she's as professional as I think she is . . .'

There was a silence, while everybody looked at Rose, and Rose looked at the carpet.

'I'll tell you what.' Mrs French crossed to the door. 'I'll go and make us all a cup of coffee, while Rose sits here and has a think. I'm sure when she's done so she'll realize that things aren't anywhere near as bad as they seem. It's simply a question of changing one part for another. Nothing so very catastrophic.' She held open the door, looking at Nicola as she did so. 'Coming?'

Nicola jumped up, gladly: she was only too pleased to escape. She followed Mrs French down a passage and into a large, Aladdin's cave of a kitchen, with stone flags on the floor and a sink the size of a bath tub, with two of the most enormous taps she had ever seen. In the middle of the flags stood a wooden table about ninety feet long – well, say fifty feet long – at any rate, a great deal longer than the table in Mrs Bruce's kitchen. This table wouldn't even fit *into* Mrs Bruce's kitchen. Mrs French pressed a switch attached to something which looked like a large thermos flask.

'Tell me –' she began unhooking mugs from a row of hooks on the wall '– does Rose always get whatever she wants?'

'Yes,' said Nicola. 'Usually.'

'What about you? Do you?'

'Well –' She considered the question, trying to be fair. 'Sometimes.'

'Haven't you ever wanted to learn dancing, as Rose does?'

Nicola frowned, and ran a finger along the edge of the table. Once, ages ago – ages and *ages* ago – she had thought that perhaps she might. She had mentioned it one Christmas, when her grandparents had been there. Her grandfather, teasing, had said, 'What! A great lanky beanpole like you?' Her grandmother, trying to be kind, had told her to 'Come on, then! Show us what you can do'; but when she had, they had all laughed at her. Rose had laughed louder than anyone. Mr Bruce, afterwards, feeling sorry for her, had pulled her on to his knee for a cuddle and said, 'She might not be any good at waving her legs in the air, but she makes a smashing centre forward – don't you, me old Nickers?' She'd given up the idea of dancing classes after that. Dancing was stupid, anyhow. She'd far rather play football.

'No?' Mrs French was looking at her. Nicola hunched a shoulder. 'What made them send Rose for lessons?'

'Don't remember. 'Spect they thought she'd be good at it.'

'And they didn't think you would be?'

'S'pose not.'

'Do *you* think you would be?'

'Don't know.'

'Well, let's have a try,' said Mrs French. She suddenly left her coffee mugs and advanced upon Nicola round the table. 'How old are you?'

'Eleven,' said Nicola.

'Eleven and how much?'

'Eleven years and two months.'

'Right. So let's see what you're like on flexibility . . . if I support you, how far back can you bend?'

Nicola didn't need support – she could bend as far back as anyone wanted her to. She could go right over and touch the floor. But that wasn't dancing, that was gymnastics. She was quite good at gymnastics. She could turn somersaults and do the splits and walk on her hands, and all sorts of things.

'What about frog's legs?' said Mrs French. 'Stretch out on the – no, wait! It'll be cold. Lie on this –' she snatched a coat off a peg and spread it out. 'Lie on your back, as flat as you can . . . that's it. Now, put the soles of your feet together and bend your legs outwards as far as they'll go, making sure your knees are touching the floor . . . that's not bad at all! Quite a lot of natural turn out. What are your feet like?'

'Just feet,' said Nicola, bewildered. Even Rose didn't have special sort of feet. At least, she didn't think she had. She was sure her mother would have mentioned it if she had.

Mrs French laughed.

'Don't look so worried, I'm not looking for extra toes – though if the first three did happen by any chance to be more or less the same length, it would be a distinct advantage. Makes point work far easier. Let's have a look. Come on! Up on the table and get your socks off . . . mm, well, two the same length. Good high arches. Any trouble with your ankles?'

Nicola shook her head. This was all very strange. She was sure Madam Paula had never made Rose sit on a table and take her socks off.

The door opened and the curly black head that belonged to Mr French peered round. At the sight of Nicola, bare-footed amongst the coffee mugs, he groaned and said, 'Why is it one can never get away from feet in this house?'

'Because feet are important.' Mrs French handed Nicola her socks back. 'I'm glad to say that Nicola's passed the test with flying colours.'

'Bully for Nicola . . . can I scrounge a coffee?'

'Oh, God, I forgot about it!' Mrs French flew back across the room to the thermos flask. 'Nicola, I didn't ask you . . . do you drink coffee, or would you rather have milk?'

'Rose has milk,' said Nicola.

'How about you?'

'I don't mind what I have.'

'Spoken bravely,' said Mr French.

They went back to the front room to find Rose still red-faced and tearful but at least no longer weeping.

'I've been telling her,' said Mrs Bruce. 'She's still got her audition to look forward to. She might well get something from that.'

'Indeed she might,' said Mrs French. 'And then think how grand she'd be . . . we'd have to count ourselves lucky if she even passed the time of day with us!'

Rose puckered her lips, to indicate that she knew very well she was only being humoured. She didn't join in any of the conversation which followed, but kept her head bent over her mug of warm milk, not even looking up when Nicola, rather shyly, asked Mrs French what it had been like to be a soloist with the Royal Ballet. Mrs French shook her head.

'I'm afraid I was only a very minor soloist . . . I never aspired to the Lilac Fairy or Queen of the Wilis, or anything like that. Peasant pas-de-deux from *Giselle* was about as far as I ever got. I wasn't really the right physical type. My thighs were always too fat, and my knees were too knobbly.'

'I can hardly believe *that*,' protested Mrs Bruce.

'Oh, I promise you, it's quite true . . . they may not look particularly fat or knobbly just at this moment, but put them under a tutu and you'd soon see what I mean! One really needs legs like Nicola's – nice and long and straight.'

Nicola had never given much thought to her legs. She knew that they were long, because her mother always said she would make a good wading bird, and sometimes she'd heard people describe her as gangling. She hadn't known that they were *nice* and long – or that they were straight. She glanced at them, now, surreptitiously, as they hung down over the edge of the leather chair. They just looked like ordinary legs to her. Her mother also glanced at them, not quite so surreptitiously.

'Nicola's legs are too thin,' she said. 'Make her look like a crane.'

'Well, it's better than looking like a female hammer thrower . . . female hammer throwers don't get anywhere; not in ballet. Cranes sometimes do.'

Mrs Bruce didn't say anything to that. There was a pause, then she leaned forward to place her mug back on the tray.

'Come along, you two. It's time we were off.' She took Rose's half-empty mug away from her. 'We've imposed on Mrs French quite long enough.'

'You haven't imposed at all,' said Mrs French. 'I'm glad that you came. I just hope we see both Nicola *and* Rose at our next rehearsal – oh, and by the way, you may be getting a call from our wardrobe mistress some time during the week. She wants to come round and measure up for costumes. I gave her your number. I hope that was all right?'

'Of course. Though whether they'll both – well! We shall have to see. Nicola, if you're taking that book, you make sure you look after it.'

They walked back up the road in silence, Mrs Bruce in the lead, Nicola, clutching her book and thinking about her legs (nice and long . . . *and* straight) a few paces behind, and Rose, who usually skipped and hopped and danced about, morosely dragging her feet in the rear. As they reached the house, Mrs Bruce, holding the gate, said, 'Well?' It seemed to be directed at Nicola. It couldn't really be directed at anyone else – Rose was still trailing, several yards behind. Nicola looked at her mother, warily.

'Well what?'

'You're determined not to let Rose have her part back again?'

'It's not her part.' Jealously, she hugged *Theatre Street* to her chest. Mrs French had lent it to *her*, just as she'd given the part of the Bad Little Girl to her. 'It's my part.'

'It *was* Rose's before.'

No, it wasn't, thought Nicola. It was always mine. She walked through the gate.

'She can do the other one – the one they're writing in for her.'

'I won't!' Rose's voice came shrilly from somewhere outside in the road. 'If I can't do the part I want, I won't do any!'

Under cover of the darkness, Nicola pulled one of her squint-eyed faces and stuck out her tongue; then she turned, and stumped off up the path. If Rose wanted to cut herself out entirely, then that was her problem.

6

The problem may have been Rose's, but Rose being Rose the rest of the house were not denied their share in it. Someone had only to mention the word ballet, or dance – or even just *performance* – for the tears to come spurting. For three whole days she walked round red-eyed, with a wet handkerchief permanently screwed into a ball, and at mealtimes sat in silence, toying with her food and saying, 'No, I couldn't, it'd make me *ill*,' when exhorted by Mrs Bruce to try and eat something. She wouldn't talk to Nicola at all. She wouldn't even say please or thank you, or ask her to pass the salt, let alone make any sort of conversation.

Nicola tried hard to tell herself that *she* didn't care – she wouldn't care if Rose never addressed another word to her as long as she lived – she didn't even *like* Rose; but it was difficult, when it was your own sister, and you not only had to live under the same roof but go to the same school and walk the same corridors. It was difficult not to be affected by it. One way and another, there was so much reproach being cast round that it quite soured any personal triumph she might have felt. Mrs Bruce had said her piece and didn't intend saying any more: *she* just looked, and occasionally pursed her lips. But then Mr Bruce, too, felt the need to join in. He was waiting in the hall one morning, as Nicola came clumping back in her gum boots after taking Ben for his walk.

'Tell me,' he said, 'this part you're doing – the one that

Rose was going to do . . . means a lot to you, does it?'

Nicola frowned.

'Mrs French asked me to do it.'

'Yes, I know she did. I was just wondering . . . how much it meant to you? Whether it was really all that important?'

Nicola concentrated on removing her gum boots before she could be accused of treading mud into the carpet. How could she explain that it wasn't the part in *itself* which was so important – though the part was fun, of course. She enjoyed conjuring up imaginary mice and pulling rude faces, and she rather thought she was going to enjoy doing it in front of an audience as well; but what was more important was the fact that Mrs French had wanted *her*. *Her* instead of *Rose*. That was what was really important. Nobody, in the whole of her life, had ever preferred her to Rose before.

Her silence obviously made Mr Bruce uncomfortable: he never liked having to speak seriously to her about anything.

'I just thought I'd ask.' He ruffled her hair with clumsy affection. 'Don't you worry about it. It's your part, you go ahead and do it. Rose will get over it. Not the end of the world.'

On Saturday afternoon the wardrobe mistress came round to take measurements. Her name was Miss Harris, and she reminded Nicola, rather unpleasantly, of a teacher she had once had at primary school. The teacher had been thin and waspish, with big globular eyes, and had disliked Nicola from the word go. Miss Harris didn't have globular eyes, but she was certainly thin and waspish. Furthermore, she was most put out when she discovered that it was Nicola she had come to measure and not Rose.

'Where's the other one?' (Her voice was *definitely* waspish.) 'The little one, with the freckles? I thought she was the one that was doing it.'

Mrs Bruce looked at Nicola rather hard.

'She was doing it, until Mrs French changed the parts around.'

'Oh? So what part is she playing now? I didn't know there *were* any other parts. I thought I'd already measured for them all. What part is she playing?'

'She isn't,' said Mrs Bruce, 'any more.'

Miss Harris made an irritable clicking noise.

'It would help if they'd keep a person informed . . . I've gone ahead and chosen all the materials now. Arranged all the colour schemes.' From out of a large plastic carrier bag she pulled a length of buttercup yellow material. 'This would have suited the other little girl beautifully. I don't know how it's going to look on this one.'

'Yellow doesn't really suit Nicola,' said Mrs Bruce.

'No, it doesn't. She's far too sallow.' Miss Harris draped the material over Nicola's shoulder and turned her towards the light. She tutted again, impatiently. 'It's going to make her look as if she's got jaundice.'

'That's what I've always found,' said Mrs Bruce. 'I never buy her anything in yellow if I can help it. Or pink. Blues and browns suit her best.'

'Well, she can't have either blue *or* brown, I'm afraid. They wouldn't go with my colour scheme. It'll have to be the yellow . . . my goodness! You are a skinny one! Where's your waist? You don't seem to have any.'

Nicola was affronted. Of course she had a waist! It was there, in the middle of her body, the same as everyone else's. What was the woman talking about?

'I suppose this must be it, here.' Resigned, Miss Harris wrapped a tape measure round her. 'There isn't any difference between your waist and your hips. I shall have to bulk you out. It doesn't matter so much about the top half, but you've got to have *some* shape . . . what are you going to do about your hair?'

Nicola looked instinctively at her mother for guidance. Mrs Bruce sighed.

'I never know *what* to do about Nicola's hair.'

'It ought to be long, if it's Victorian. That's another expense . . . I'll have to hire a wig – unless we could get away with a hair piece.' Miss Harris picked up a handful of Nicola's hair and regarded it doubtfully. 'Hm! There's not much of it, is there?'

'I try to keep it fairly short,' said Mrs Bruce. 'It looks better that way.'

'Yes; it would.' Miss Harris, disparagingly, let the hair fall back where it belonged, on top of Nicola's head. 'No body, that's the trouble.' Rose's hair, of course, had plenty of body. It sprang about all over the place. Even when it was wet it was all thick and bunchy. When Nicola's was wet it just clung limply about her face in hanks. 'Oh, well!' Miss Harris squared her shoulders. 'We shall just have to do the best we can.'

From the tone of her voice, it didn't seem that she held out much hope of the best being anything very satisfactory. Nicola began to feel like an undersized chicken that wasn't even fit to have its neck wrung.

'I suppose they must know what they're about.' Miss Harris grumbled to herself as she took down measurements. 'They wouldn't switch parts for no reason. I must say, the other little one always looked all right to me, but then I'm only wardrobe. Nobody ever considers wardrobe. First they expect you to operate on a shoestring –'

Shoestring? thought Nicola. What on earth was a shoestring? Did she mean shoelaces? Perhaps when she'd been young people *did* tie their shoes with bits of string. Come to think of it, they probably did. Shoelaces most likely wouldn't have been invented at the turn of the century. She still didn't see how you could *operate* on one. She came to the conclusion that Miss Harris was loopy. What with not knowing where people's waists were, and then thinking that someone wanted her to operate on a tiny bit of string . . .

'It's always the same.' Miss Harris grumbled on. 'They

seem to think you can work miracles. They've got no idea how much things *cost* these days.'

Mrs Bruce nodded, sympathetically.

'They ought to try buying school uniforms – they'd learn soon enough. You take a simple thing like a blazer –'

Miss Harris wasn't interested in simple things like blazers. She seized Nicola's hand and crossly jerked her arm out straight.

'Materials have gone up and up – and *then* there's all the sewing to be done. They don't take into account the reels of cotton one has to buy. Keep still, child, and don't wriggle! How can I measure you if you're moving about all the time? In future, I shall tell them, you go to a theatrical costumier. It's all very well, saying they want to build up their own wardrobe, but who has to do all the work? I wouldn't mind if they'd just keep me informed. But when they go round changing parts at a moment's notice –'

Nobody (except, presumably, Miss Harris) ever knew what happened when they went round changing parts at a moment's notice, because at this point the door crashed open and an apparition burst in. Miss Harris broke off in mid-grievance. She stared, slack-jawed, across the room. Nicola and Mrs Bruce also stared. The apparition stood and simpered. It was wearing a pink net party frock and had its face plastered in make-up, the mouth a red gash, the eyes bright green surrounded by thick rings of black, some of which had smudged and transferred itself to neighbouring portions of the face. A strong aroma of perfume filled the air.

'What on *earth* –' Mrs Bruce took a step forward. 'Is that my Chanel you've been at?'

For just a second, the apparition showed signs of uncertainty. The simper faltered – as well it might, thought Nicola. She was awed, in spite of herself. Mrs Bruce's Chanel was more precious than the Crown Jewels. More

precious than *gold* dust. It had been a present from Mr Bruce
on their last wedding anniversary. It was in the tiniest bottle
that anyone had ever seen, and Mrs Bruce had told them
repeatedly that 'If I catch *either* of you, *ever*, touching my
Chanel –'

'My goodness!' cried Miss Harris. She giggled. 'It does
smell nice!'

Confidence reasserted itself: the apparition broke into a
happy beam.

'Rose, this is not funny!'

Mrs Bruce, all too obviously, was not finding it so; neither
was Nicola. It was the first time she could ever remember
that Rose had really done something awful. It didn't seem
right, coming from Rose. Nicola was the one that did the
awful things: she was the one that got slapped and told off
and had her pocket money stopped. This was turning
everything topsy turvy. Only Miss Harris still seemed to find
it funny. Even Rose had stopped beaming and was
beginning to quiver. Mrs Bruce advanced upon her
wrathfully.

'How much have you used? Half the bottle, from the
smell of you!'

'I should think she's bathed in it,' said Miss Harris. She
giggled again. 'At least she's got good taste!'

Mrs Bruce was too cross to be amused. Nicola could see
that she was cross – her lips had gone all pinched and her
cheeks were sucked in. When that happened, it meant
trouble. Nicola had observed it all too often.

'How many times have I told you that you are *not* to touch
my Chanel? And what's that make-up doing, smeared all
over your face? Where did you get it from? Out of my
bedroom! You have no *right* to go into my bedroom, helping
yourself to my things. Look at the mess you've made! You've
got lipstick all over that frock. If you've got it on my
bedroom carpet, I'm warning you, there's going to be

70

trouble. What for goodness' sake did you think you were doing?'

To this, Rose made no reply – probably couldn't, thought Nicola, from the depths of her own experience. Already the tears had come gushing. Two black rivulets were slowly rolling down the rouged cheeks, leaving dirty trails behind them. Nicola turned away, not liking to look. She knew what Rose had thought she was doing: she had thought she was making an impression on Miss Harris. She had thought Miss Harris was going to turn round and say, 'Oh! What a dear little girl! We *must* have her back in the show instead of the other one.' She hadn't got the least idea that she looked ridiculous. She'd done her eyes like Mrs French did hers – *tried* to do her eyes like Mrs French did hers – and put on her best dress and come prancing downstairs without a doubt in the world but that she was going to be crooned over. Nothing else could have given her the courage to drench herself in Chanel – although, upon reflection, it probably hadn't been a question of courage, with Rose. Rose was always so sure of herself – always so *sure* that she was pretty, so *sure* that everyone was going to approve of her – that very likely she'd just have gone marching straight in and helped herself without even giving it a second thought.

Nicola watched, in awed silence, as a weeping Rose was led away. For once in her life, she was glad she wasn't in Rose's shoes. Pinching Mrs Bruce's Chanel was almost the worst thing that either of them had ever done. (Not that Rose ever *did*.) It was far worse than just smashing windows or setting light to the fence. It was even worse than when Nicola had scrubbed the dining room table with bleach and taken all the polish off. At least on that occasion she'd had the quite genuine excuse that she thought she was helping – she'd only been six years old. You didn't know any better at six years old. Rose was ten, and certainly knew better.

She wondered if she felt like gloating. She tried a few

71

gloating thoughts, by way of experiment . . . *Rose*, getting whacked . . . *Rose*, getting told off . . . *Rose*, having her pocket money stopped . . . Somehow, the gloat wouldn't come. All she could think of was Rose standing there looking ridiculous with eye make-up running all over her face.

'Well!' Miss Harris seemed in better humour than she had before. 'What a little monkey! That's what I should call a *really* bad little girl.' She laughed, tinnily, as she ran the tape measure down Nicola's leg. 'Good gracious, child, you're all limbs!'

Nicola glowered beneath her lashes. What did she mean, all limbs? She only had four, didn't she, the same as other people? And Rose *wasn't* bad. Nicola was the one that was bad. That was why Mrs French had wanted her.

'I wonder,' mused Miss Harris, 'if we might be able to get you a *blond* wig? Anything to make you look less sallow . . . it's a pity you haven't got your sister's colouring. We could have got away without make-up, with her. You're definitely going to need something on those cheeks, especially standing right next to Mark. He's such a very *fair* little boy. You're not going to look a bit like brother and sister. Still –' she rolled up her tape measure and with an air of fatalism stowed it away in the plastic bag '– I suppose they must know what they're doing.'

Mrs Bruce came back, looking flustered.

'Honestly! That's nearly half a bottle of expensive perfume gone. I simply cannot imagine what came over her.'

'Oh, they get the devil in them at times.' Miss Harris spoke with the air of one who knows. 'We can't expect them to be little angels.'

'Well, I wouldn't say that Rose is a little angel, but she's certainly never done anything like this before. I can only excuse her on the grounds that she has been very upset just lately. It came as quite a shock when Mrs French suddenly decided to take the part away from her like that – she's been sobbing her heart out for the last three days. The poor child couldn't understand what she's supposed to have done wrong.'

'She didn't do anything wrong,' said Nicola, 'she just wasn't *bad* enough.'

'Well! Not bad enough!' Miss Harris echoed the words, with another of her tinny laughs. 'I've never heard that one before!'

'She was supposed,' said Nicola, 'to be playing a bad little girl.'

'It seems to me, she is a bad little girl!'

'She's not as a rule,' said Mrs Bruce. 'She's usually good as gold. As a matter of fact, I'm really rather worried about her. She hasn't eaten anything for –'

'Oh, if she wants the part as badly as all that she might as well *have* it.' Nicola stalked across the room. '*I* don't care.' She tore open the door. 'I didn't really want it, anyway.'

'Nicola!' Her mother's voice stopped her as she was half way up the stairs. 'Come back a minute . . . I want a word with you.'

If she was going to have a go at her for being *rude* –

'Come on!'

Sulkily, Nicola went back down.

'Did you really mean that?' said Mrs Bruce. 'About letting Rose take over the part again?'

No . . . *no*! She didn't really mean it, she shouldn't ever have said it, it was *her* part, Mrs French had given it to *her* –

'Did you?' said Mrs Bruce.

Nicola clenched her fists tight behind her back. She nodded.

'Are you quite sure? It's not something you're going to regret?'

She was already regretting it. She *hated* Rose. Rose had *every*thing.

'It would certainly make life a lot easier,' said Miss Harris.

'It would certainly make Rose a lot happier.' Mrs Bruce smiled at Nicola. 'I'll tell you what . . . as a reward, I'll buy you those running shoes you wanted. How about it? Would that please you? We might even stretch to a new top, as well, if you like. You deserve something. Suppose I meet you after school on Monday and we go down the road and have a look?'

Nicola tried to feel enthusiastic at the prospect, but it wasn't any use. She couldn't – not now. It had come too late. She'd wanted the running shoes in September. She didn't really care about them any more. She hunched a shoulder.

'All right.'

'*Thank* you,' prompted Mrs Bruce.

'*Thank* you,' said Nicola.

She supposed she should have known better than to expect any gratitude from Rose. When she went downstairs at four o'clock to have tea (having spent the past hour seeking solace in her bedroom with Ben – not that Ben was terribly good at solacing: he tended to think life was just one big joke) she found her father watching football and Rose stuffing herself with buttered crumpets.

'Where's mine?' said Nicola.

Rose beamed, greedily. She had trickles of melted butter running down her chin.

'You weren't here, so I ate them.'

'Pig!'

'You should've come earlier. They go flabby if they're left.'

'Don't want any, anyhow.'

'You'd better.' Mr Bruce spoke without taking his eyes off the football. 'Your mother's out in the kitchen right now doing some more.'

Nicola knelt down on the hearthrug with Ben. They both

74

of them looked accusingly at Rose, stuffing the last piece of crumpet into her mouth.

'You'll get fat,' said Nicola.

'No, I won't. Miss Harris said I've got a nice little shape.'

'*Yuck*.' Nicola made a being-sick noise.

'She said it was just as well I was doing the part again . . . she said you'd have looked all wrong in it.'

'She's just stupid.'

'No, she isn't.' Rose had obviously found an ally in Miss Harris. 'She said she couldn't understand why they'd ever changed the parts round in the first place . . . she's going to tell Mrs French that now I've got it back again I've got to keep it because she's going to run the costume up this evening. She says Mrs French'll probably be quite glad, secretly. After all –' Rose, with relish, licked buttery fingers '– I was the one she originally wanted.'

Nicola's face turned scarlet with indignation.

'*I* was the one she originally wanted. She wanted me *ages* before she wanted you. You've only got it back again because *I* said you could.'

Rose was not one to be easily shaken: when it came to her own self-esteem, she always had an answer ready.

'I s'pose you got cold feet. Amateurs usually do.'

The *cheek* of it. It almost took one's breath away. Nicola leaned forward and hissed furiously in Rose's face.

'If you want to know the truth, it was because I felt sorry for you, making such an *idiot* of yourself.'

'You'd have made an idiot of yourself, if you'd gone ahead and done it!'

'I jolly well wouldn't have made such an idiot of myself as you did . . . you had *eye* black all over your *face*. You looked *ridiculous*.'

'No, I didn't!'

'Yes, you did!'

'No, I –'

'For heaven's sake!' Mr Bruce snapped off the television set. 'Can't you two ever conduct a civilized conversation? Just give it a rest for five minutes!'

They subsided, glaring at each other. Ben, evidently feeling the occasion called for a comic turn, rolled over on to his back and lay there, grinning, with his legs in the air.

'That's better.' Mr Bruce picked up the *Radio Times*. 'Bit of peace and quiet for once.'

Mrs Bruce came into the room carrying the teapot and a dish full of hot buttered crumpets.

'Ah, Nicola, there you are.' She put the teapot in the hearth and the dish of crumpets on a small side table. 'Has Rose thanked you nicely for letting her have the part back?'

Nicola looked, and said nothing. Rose, with a pout, muttered something that might or might not have been 'Thank you'.

'Well! That wasn't very gracious, was it?' Mrs Bruce settled herself in an arm chair. 'Surely you can do better than that?'

Rose turned slightly pink (with vexation rather than embarrassment).

'Thank you very much,' she said, 'for letting me have the part back ... but I *was* the one they originally wanted.'

'Rose! That's quite enough. Nicola's been very generous, don't go and ruin it. Pass her the crumpets.'

Rose, with bad grace, did so. Nicola took one and dropped it without much enthusiasm on to her plate. Squidgy fat crumpet. It made her feel sick.

'Eat up, then.' Mr Bruce was watching her. 'No danger of *you* putting on weight ... you don't really mind too much about this part, do you?'

Nicola swallowed.

'Not particularly.'

'Not going to make you unhappy, is it?'

She forced back tears.

''Course not.'

'I shouldn't like to think you'd been pressurized.'

Nicola didn't know what pressurized meant. She only knew that she certainly wasn't going to let *Rose* see she cared.

'Didn't really want it, anyway. It's soppy, all that sort of thing.'

Rose's voice rang out, shrill and piercing, from the other side of the hearth, 'You won't think it's soppy when I'm famous . . . when I'm rich and on television and everybody's heard of me!'

Nicola felt a large wodge of crumpet moving slowly down the centre of her chest towards her stomach.

'Who wants to be rich and famous?' said Mr Bruce. 'There's more to life than that, you know. I'll tell you what, me old Nickers!' He leaned towards her, and tweaked companionably at her hair. 'How about you and me going down to Selhurst Park next Saturday? Eh? See Palace at home to West Ham? Should be a good game. What d'you reckon?'

He was trying to be nice to her. Nicola choked. She didn't *want* people to be nice to her – she didn't *want* to go down to Selhurst Park, she didn't *want* to see Crystal Palace at home to West Ham. All she wanted was to play the part that she had been chosen for. And now she couldn't because she'd gone and given it back to Rose, who was nothing but a mean and hateful pig and didn't deserve it.

'So how about it?' said Mr Bruce. 'Long time since we've been to a game together . . . shall we make it a date?'

Nicola pushed the remains of her crumpet towards Ben. 'S'pose we could,' she said. 'If you want.'

7

The week that followed was disastrous: everything went wrong that possibly could. Miss McMaster, in English, told her that her latest essay was 'a *sad* disappointment . . . not at all what I've come to expect of you' (she'd been too busy thinking about Mrs French and the mime show to concentrate properly on writing essays). Mr Drew, in geography, said that her map drawing was a 'most miserable effort', and that if that was the best she could do she had better stay in at break and trace the outline of Italy six times by way of practice. In singing she was told off for making up what Miss Murray called 'stupid and ridiculous words' to the song they were supposed to be singing – instead of *Sleep on a little while, and in thy slumber smile,* Nicola had sung, *Sleep on a wooden door, and in thy slumber snore,* which everybody else had thought quite funny, but Miss Murray notoriously had no sense of humour. She had said that if Nicola persisted in such juvenile behaviour, she would have no option but to report her. Finally, just to round off the week, she had been sent out of an RI class by Miss Joyce for being 'impertinent and unwholesome'; and while she was standing under the clock in the front hall, which was where sinners were traditionally sent to stand, Mr Henry had come out of his study and said, 'Good heavens alive, Nicola! Not you again?' Her form mistress had said that if there was any more of it, she would seriously have to consider talking to her parents. 'I hear nothing but reports of how you refuse to cooperate, or how you've been a disruptive influence. It really isn't good enough, Nicola. You're a bright child – why can't you behave like one?'

Because she didn't want to, that was why. She didn't want to be a bright child, she wanted to be a stupid, pretty, fussed-over, *spoilt* child. She wanted to be a child who always got what she wanted. You didn't get what you wanted by sometimes coming top in exams or being given good marks for essays. Nobody cared about that sort of thing. If Rose went home and said that Madam Paula had told her her pirouettes were the best in the whole class, Mrs Bruce would instantly stop whatever she was doing and demand to be shown the wonderful pirouettes there and then; but if Nicola went home and said she'd got nine out of ten for an essay and offered to read it aloud, it was, 'That would be lovely, let's wait till I can really sit down and concentrate,' only she never *did* sit down and concentrate because she didn't really *care*. Nobody cared. And if nobody cared, then she couldn't see that it mattered whether she behaved like a bright child or an idiot child, or even like a juvenile delinquent, if that was how she felt. She would behave exactly as she wanted to behave.

On Saturday morning, when Rose had gone to her tap dancing class, she took Ben for a walk.

'Just remember,' said Mrs Bruce, 'you keep away from that building site.'

Why should she keep away from the building site? She liked the building site. She'd go on a *million* building sites, if that was what she wanted.

Defiant in blue jeans and her gum boots, Nicola stumped up the road and clambered over the earth mound into the mud. Ben slithered joyously at her side – he was already caked all over with clay. He lumbered out of the ditch and shook himself, vigorously: filthy droplets spattered Nicola's sweater. It was the new sweater which she had been bought

79

as a reward for being nice to Rose. Five seconds ago, it had been snowy white, with red ribbing at the waist and cuffs; now it was more a kind of dirty grey, with brown blobs speckled over it. Mrs Bruce had been doubtful at the time as to the wisdom of buying anything white. Rose had white: Nicola was more a brown and navy type. She had only given way because Nicola for once in her life had been good and deserved a special treat. She was going to be furious when she saw the state she had got herself in.

Nicola scowled. So what? It was her sweater. If she wanted it to be a dirty grey, then it was no one's business but hers.

She played for a while on the mound, while Ben went splashing off on his own. She tried singing rude songs about Rose – Rose, Rose, wobbling on her toes, Falling in the mud on her big red nose – but somehow the game had lost its charm. It wasn't as much fun as it had been. She had just abandoned the rude songs in favour of seeing whether she could jump the ditch at its widest point, when a voice called out to her from the other side of the earth works. *Splat*, went Nicola; straight into the mud. She hauled herself out and slopped boggily across the sea of clay.

'My goodness!' said Mrs French. 'You are in a mess!'

So what? They were her clothes, weren't they? It was her skin. If she *wanted* to get herself into a mess –

'I was very sorry,' said Mrs French, 'to hear that you won't be playing the part for us after all . . . I'd rather been hoping this was one occasion when Rose *wouldn't* get her own way. They didn't make you feel guilty about it, did they? It wouldn't be fair if they did. After all, Rose *was* offered something else.'

'She wouldn't do it,' said Nicola.

'So you had to sacrifice your part? That doesn't seem right.'

Nicola struggled for a moment with self pity.

'Didn't really bother me.' She stuck her thumbs into the

80

back pockets of her jeans and took up an aggressive stance, legs apart, chin tilted. 'Didn't really care all that much.'

'Didn't you?' said Mrs French. 'I thought you looked as if you were thoroughly enjoying it that one night.'

Tears pricked at the back of Nicola's eyes. She stubbed the toe of her gum boot into the mud.

'It was all right.'

'I see. So you're not desperately upset about not being in it?'

'Not upset at all. I'm going to see Crystal Palace play West Ham.'

'Are you, indeed? You like football, do you?'

'It's better than dancing . . . dancing's wet.'

Mrs French pulled just the slightest of faces.

'I'm afraid I don't know anything about football. What is it? A cup tie, or something?'

'*League*,' said Nicola. She couldn't altogether keep a note of scorn out of her voice. Cup tie! Where would Mr Bruce be likely to get tickets for a cup tie? Anyhow, Crystal Palace was already out. They'd gone out in the first round.

'Well! Let's hope it's a good match,' said Mrs French.

She smiled, and went on her way. Nicola was left by herself to do battle against a sudden and terrible desire to burst into tears. She mustn't – she *wouldn't*. Crying was ignoble. Crying was what Rose always resorted to. Nicola was tough: *she* didn't cry.

'Hi, Nickers!'

Nicola looked up, and through a faint blur saw three of the boys from her class at school – Kevin Batchelor, Denny Waters and Terry Pitsea. They weren't particular friends of hers, though sometimes, as a mark of respect, they let her kick a football around with them. Kevin had once said that she was almost like a boy, and 'heaps better than that stupid sister of yours'.

''Lo.' She turned and whistled at Ben, as an excuse to hide

81

her face until all traces of possible tears might be gone. Nicola could whistle by putting two fingers in her mouth, a feat of which she was justifiably proud. Not even Kevin could whistle like that. She whistled a second time, just for good measure. Ben, needless to say, took not the slightest bit of notice, but at least the tears had dried up. She turned back again. 'Didn't know you lived round here?'

'Bin to see someone.'

"Cept they wasn't in.' Terry scrambled up the earthworks to join her. 'What you doin'?'

'Nothing special.'

'That your dog?'

Nicola looked, and saw Ben on his back, energetically rolling. She nodded.

'What's 'is name?'

'Ben.'

'Come 'ere, Ben!' Kevin, jumping up beside Terry, snapped his fingers. Ben went on rolling. 'Any good at doin' tricks, is 'e?'

'He can beg,' said Nicola. 'Sort of. Sometimes,' she added.

'Does 'e sit, an' stay, an' all that sort o' thing?'

'I expect he would, if he was trained.'

'Let's train 'im now . . . sit, Ben.' Kevin pointed sternly to the ground. Ben stood up and wagged his tail. 'Sit . . . well, stay, then . . . *stay* . . . there! 'E's stayed. I know a thing or two about dogs, I do. Got one o' me own. All right, Ben, now you c'n sit . . . *sit* . . . e's not quite sure of it yet, 'e thinks it means lie down.'

"E thinks it means roll,' said Terry. 'What is 'e, anyway? Sort o' sheepdog, or something?'

'He's a mongrel,' said Nicola.

'They're the best,' said Kevin. 'Look, 'e's learnt already . . . 'e's sittin'. Good boy, Ben! Good boy!'

A small, virtuous voice suddenly piped up from the road

outside, 'You'll catch it, you will, playing on that building site.' It was Rose, self-important, on her way home from Madam Paula's. Nicola stuck her tongue out: Kevin put two fingers in the air.

'You just wait,' said Rose.

She trotted on down the road, her hair (full of body) bouncing self-righteously behind her as she went. Denny jerked a contemptuous thumb over his shoulder.

'What's her problem?'

'I'm not meant to play here,' said Nicola. 'She'll be mad when she finds out.'

'Who? Your mum?'

Nicola nodded, gloomily. Rose was bound to tell. It would be the first thing she said, the minute she got indoors: 'I saw Nicola playing on the building site . . .' She grabbed Ben by the collar and snapped on his lead before he could make a break for freedom.

'Let's go somewhere else.'

'Where?'

'We could go up the Common,' said Terry.

'I'm sick o' the Common.' Kevin heaved a lump of rock: it fell with a satisfying *plash* into the ditch full of muddy water. 'Let's *do* somethin'.'

'Let's go and steal a chicken,' said Nicola.

They stared at her; impressed, but wondering.

'Where from?' said Kevin.

'Butcher up the road. He's got hundreds of them, all lying about.'

'But what we stealin' it *for*?' said Denny.

'Steal it for your mum.'

She knew that Denny's mum liked chickens because Denny had written an essay about it which Miss McMaster had read out to the class on the same day that she had told Nicola her work was 'a sad disappointment'. Denny's mum had had a sad disappointment. She had saved up her money for a whole fortnight in order to buy a chicken to make some special West Indian dish for Denny's brother's birthday, and on the way home in the bus her shopping bag had been stolen, so that instead of having chicken for his birthday Denny's brother had had to have a boiled egg, and his mum had made a joke about it and said that instead of having chicken *roast* they were having chicken *boiled* (a joke which some of the dimmer members of the class, having apparently quite forgotten that chickens came out of eggs, had had to have explained to them).

'I ain't never stolen nothin' before,' said Denny.

'Neither have I,' said Nicola. Stealing was wicked: she suddenly felt excited. 'Wouldn't your mum *like* a chicken?'

'Yeah, but –'

'Denny's chicken,' said Terry; and doubled up laughing at his own wit. 'D'yer get it? Denny's chicken 'cos he's scared to steal a chicken –'

'Even for his own mum,' said Nicola.

'I don't want to get into no trouble,' said Denny.

'You won't get into trouble: *I'll* get into trouble. *I'll* steal the chicken and you can just stand and watch . . . come on!' Nicola jumped over the earth works on to the pavement. Now that she'd had the idea, she wanted to put it into practice. 'All those who aren't chicken, follow me!'

Terry ranged himself at her elbow; Kevin, who always liked to be the leader in any joint endeavours, strode a few paces ahead; Denny, still reluctant, brought up the rear. They cut across Fenning Road, went up a side street to avoid any possibility of bumping into Mrs Bruce, and turned into Streatham High Road.

'Where's this butcher, then?'

'Further down. He's all hidden away by himself. Be easy as pie.'

The butcher may have been all hidden away by himself – he was one of four shops in a tiny passage called Islet Court

84

– but Nicola had forgotten that it was Saturday morning. The shop was crowded with customers, all pushing and cramming. Obviously impossible, even for someone as thin as herself, to wriggle her way through to the front, snatch a chicken from the window, and wriggle out again without being caught.

'So now what we gonna do?' Kevin's voice was challenging. He looked pointedly at Nicola as they stood in a bunch on the opposite side of the road. 'Thought you said it'd be easy as pie?'

Various desperate possibilities flashed across Nicola's brain. She was about to suggest hurling a brick through the window (except that she knew that, when it came to it, she wouldn't dare. Stealing a chicken was one thing: breaking a window was quite another) when Terry, pointing, said, 'What about one o' them?' At the entrance to the butcher's, hanging from a hook, were some brownish-coloured birds with bright tail feathers, vivid blues and greens and reds. They certainly weren't chickens, but they were, presumably, meant for eating.

'What are they?' said Kevin.

Painstakingly, Terry spelt out the hand-written notice propped beneath them.

'*Peasants?*'

'Pheasants,' said Nicola. 'Like in photographs.'

Kevin turned to Denny.

'Your ole lady fancy a pheasant, Den?'

Denny's face was troubled.

'I dunno about no pheasants . . . she never said nothin' about no pheasants. Let's go, man!'

'Can't,' said Kevin. 'Not till ole Nickers's nicked somethin'.'

'Only reason we come 'ere,' said Terry. 'What's the matter? You still chicken?'

'I don't want no trouble.' Denny repeated the words

obstinately. 'I already bin in trouble once. You ain't.'

'I bin in trouble!'

'Not with the pigs, you ain't.'

'Look, shuddup!' said Kevin, fiercely. 'It's Nickers what's doin' it, not you.'

'Well, she jus' better get a move on, else I'm goin'.'

Everybody turned to look at Nicola.

'Go on, then,' said Kevin.

Nicola swallowed. Now that it had come to the point, she was rather beginning to think that she might be a bit chicken herself. She had just remembered that Mr Archer, who stood behind the counter in his striped apron, hacking up the joints of meat with his meat axe, sometimes delivered things to Fenning Road in his van. He sometimes even delivered things to Mrs Bruce. He would know who Nicola was – he would know where she lived –

'Well? Go on!' Kevin was growing impatient. 'You gonna nick a pheasant for Denny's mum or aincher?'

'Yes.' Nicola felt a surge of defiance. From now on, she was going to do just exactly whatever she wanted, no matter *how* wicked it was. In fact, the more wicked, the better.

'What about Ben?' That was Terry, showing sudden and rather belated concern. 'Want me to stay 'ere and 'old 'im?'

'Tie 'im to the lamp post.' Kevin snatched at the lead. ''E'll like that. Dogs go for lamp posts.'

The die was cast. Three abreast, they marched across the road, leaving Ben secured to his lamp post, Denny hovering at a safe distance.

''Ang about,' said Kevin. 'Someone's comin'.'

He bent, elaborately, to do up his shoelace as one of Mr Archer's assistants came walking out to the front of the shop. Calmly, the assistant unhooked a couple of pheasants, cast a casual glance at the three children standing on the pavement, and went back inside.

'There y'are,' said Terry. 'Piece o' cake.'

'Wanna leg up?' Kevin cupped his hands together. 'We'll give yer one two three . . . OK? You ready, Tel? One – two – *three* –'

Nicola found herself suddenly thrust up into the air. Wobbling perilously, she made a snatch at the nearest pheasant: the pheasant remained firmly attached to its hook. Nicola struggled, began to overbalance, and clutched in her panic at the entire bunch. As she did so, a voice came booming from inside the shop, 'What the blazes do you kids think you're up to out there?'

Kevin and Terry didn't wait to offer explanations: with one accord, they dropped Nicola and ran. Denny ran with them. Nicola was left, dangling two feet above the pavement, her hands full of dead pheasant. Across the road, Ben barked excitedly. Ben would: he was that sort of a dog.

'Well, well!' Two brawny hands reached up and plucked Nicola out of the air. She was set down with a bump on the pavement, at Mr Archer's feet. 'I seem to recognize you, young lady . . . number nine Fenning Road, if I'm not much mistaken? I think you and I had better pay a little visit to your mother . . .'

'I don't know, Nicola.' Mrs Bruce came back from closing the front door behind Mr Archer. Her voice sounded weary. 'I just do not know what we're to do with you.'

Nicola eyed her mother uncertainly. She had braced herself for a scene – a really big, unpleasant sort of scene; the sort of scene that only came once in a lifetime. Stealing was so absolutely and utterly the worst crime that she had ever committed (eclipsing a hundred times Rose's raid on the Chanel, which now seemed almost puny in comparison) that she would not have been surprised if she'd been put on bread and water and shut up in her room for a week.

'I suppose there's no point in asking what made you do it?'

'It was just a sort of – joke, really.'

'*Joke?*'

'Well . . . a sort of game. We couldn't think of anything else to do.'

'I see.' Mrs Bruce compressed her lips into a thin line. 'You couldn't think of anything else to do – *and* you've been playing on that building site again. Even though I specifically told you not to. Well, from now on your father can deal with you. As soon as he gets in from shopping I intend to have a word with him; what happens next is between him and you. I've done my share. I can't do any more. It's about time he shouldered some of the responsibility.'

Mrs Bruce left the room. A few seconds later, Nicola heard the sound of saucepans rattling in the kitchen. She stood a moment, undecided. She had been prepared for bread and water – she had even been prepared for the police. It wouldn't be the first time Mrs Bruce had threatened her – 'I'll get the police to you, my girl, if you don't mend your ways.' She had been prepared for almost anything except having her father brought into it. Mr Bruce never intervened in domestic affairs. He was the one that went out to work and earned a living: Mrs Bruce was the one who did all the telling off and the managing.

With dragging step, Nicola trailed up the stairs, with Ben, to her bedroom. Her sole consolation was that at least Rose wasn't there to gloat over her. Rose had gone across the road to play with a friend: Mr Bruce had gone to get a hair cut and buy some new bits for his electric drill. She wondered what would happen when he came back – whether he would be very angry with her. She could hardly ever remember him being angry; not really *toweringly* angry like Mrs Bruce sometimes was. He would almost certainly tell her that this afternoon was cancelled. He wouldn't be taking her to Selhurst Park to see Palace; not now. He might never take her again. He might even *beat* her. Mr Bruce had never

89

raised a finger to either of the girls – he left that sort of thing
to Mrs Bruce. Mrs Bruce quite often dealt out a sharp slap or
a box round the ears, and had once, when Nicola was little,
chased her round the garden and half way up the stairs with
a stick. She didn't *think* that Mr Bruce would do that; but she
couldn't be sure.

At midday she heard the front gate click, and peering
cautiously out of the left-hand window saw the familiar
figure of her father, in his weekend tweedy jacket and brown
trousers. He was carrying a small package, which was
presumably his new drill bits, and had an expression of
happy anticipation on his face. Nicola suddenly felt sorry for
him: *he* wasn't to know that in only a matter of seconds he
was going to be confronted by the awful news that his elder
daughter was a thief. He thought that he was going to sit
down, as usual on a Saturday, to one of Mrs Bruce's
casserole stews, followed by rhubarb pie and custard,
followed by a trip to Selhurst Park to watch Crystal Palace at
home to West Ham. Two stray tears trickled mournfully
down Nicola's cheek: why did she always have to go and
ruin things for everyone?

Ben, who had also heard the front gate, was already at the
bedroom door vociferously demanding to be let out. She
opened the door and he was off, bounding down the stairs
to give Mr Bruce the sort of greeting that might have been
thought more appropriate for someone who had been away
a whole month instead of a mere couple of hours. Nicola
watched, over the banisters. She saw her mother come up
the hall – saw her say something to Mr Bruce. It was too low
for her to hear, but she was almost certain she saw her
mother's lips form the word 'Nicola'. Mr Bruce's happy
expression changed to one of glum apprehension. Together
with Mrs Bruce, and Ben, he disappeared into the front
room. The door closed.

It was some while before Nicola could nerve herself to

creep downstairs to her listening post. It wasn't so much that she was scared of being discovered as that she was scared of hearing what was being said. She didn't *want* to hear – but she knew that she had to. She had to know what terrible things her father was being told.

By the time she reached the foot of the stairs he had obviously been told the most terrible thing of all: he had been told about her being a thief, and being brought home in disgrace by Mr Archer. She heard her mother's voice. The tone was slightly raised, and she spoke with an air of finality, 'I told her, from now on I wash my hands of you . . . it's between you and your father.'

There was a pause; then Mr Bruce said something, too low and rumbling for her to make out the words. Her mother's voice came back at him, sharp and accusing, 'Perhaps you'd have been happier if she *had* been a boy . . . heaven knows, you've done your best to make her one. I suppose you think that stealing pheasants from a butcher's shop is nothing but a mere boyish prank?'

'You did say she did it as a joke.'

'Joke! If that's your idea of a *joke* . . .'

'Well, I don't think it's quite as serious as all that.' Mr Bruce was obviously moving about the room: his voice kept coming and going. There was a gap, then, 'The girl's no thief. Not in the ordinary sense of the word. What's more important as far as I'm concerned is what's behind it all.'

'What's behind *any* of the things she does?'

'That,' said Mr Bruce, 'is what we have to try and find out.'

Nicola heard what sounded like a snort from her mother, then more low rumbling noises from her father, amongst which she managed to distinguish the phrases 'drawing attention to herself' and 'sure sign she's not happy'.

'I really don't see why,' said Mrs Bruce. 'We've always treated them exactly the same.'

'But have we?' Her father had come back within earshot.

91

'Haven't we tended to make far more of Rose, simply because she's the pretty one?'

'Not at all!' Mrs Bruce was indignant. 'As if I'd let a thing like that colour the way I treat them! I've treated them *exactly* the same.'

'It's still been Rose who's had all the attention . . . I mean, in the first place, why was it only her we sent off to have these dancing lessons and not Nicola, as well?'

'*I* don't know . . . I suppose at the time we couldn't afford to pay for two lots.'

'So it had to be Rose?'

'Well – yes! She was obviously the one who was going to benefit the most.'

'How do we know that Nicola mightn't have benefited, if she'd been given the chance? This Mrs French –' more rumbling: Nicola strained her ears almost to bursting point '– she seems to think pretty highly of her. Suppose she's right? Suppose the lass has got talent? And we've been crushing it all these years?'

Mrs Bruce stuck very firmly to her guns.

'She's never shown the least sign.'

'Or we've never shown the least interest?'

'She's the one that's never shown the interest . . . *she'd* far rather go off and kick a football around. The only reason she hung on to that part for as long as she did was to keep it from Rose. *She* didn't want it: she just didn't want Rose to have it.'

'I still think she should have been given the chance. We should have let her show what she can do. It wouldn't have hurt Rose, to suffer for a bit.'

'You say that *now*?' Mrs Bruce sounded bitter. 'You were the one who said you didn't like to see her so upset.'

'Oh, I admit it! I was as much at fault as anyone. I see now that I was wrong – we were *both* wrong. We should never have –'

Never have what? Nicola's ears, distended to about twice their normal size, flapped in vain against the banisters. The next words were from her mother, 'Well, I don't know . . . you may be right. Unfortunately it's a bit late in the day to do anything about it now. We can't take the part away from her a *second* time – anyway, the costumes have already been made.'

More rumbling.

'What about this audition you're taking Rose to? Couldn't she go with you to that?'

'What? You mean actually do an audition herself?' Mrs Bruce spoke doubtfully. 'I suppose she *could*.'

'Well, and why not? Why shouldn't she? You said when you went along to that *Annie* thing there were kids who couldn't even sing in tune.'

'I'm not altogether certain that Nicola can.'

'So give her a chance! She might surprise us all.'

There was a pause; then: 'Are you going to talk to her?' said Mrs Bruce.

'Yes, yes, leave it with me. I'll attend to it.'

'When?'

'Oh . . .'

Nicola could see her father humping his shoulders, in the way that he did when her mother was nagging at him to do something he didn't want to do. *When are you going to cut that grass? When are you going to change the washer on that tap? WHEN ARE YOU GOING TO TALK TO NICOLA?*

'I'll do it this afternoon,' said Mr Bruce. 'In the interval.'

'Interval? What interval?'

'Selhurst Park . . . we're going to the match. Had you forgotten?'

'Actually, I had.' Her mother's tone was dry. 'I've had rather more important matters on my mind – such as apologizing to Mr Archer. Speaking of which, I shouldn't have thought that a child who steals pheasants *deserves* to go to football matches.'

'Oh, let her be . . . she's had enough to put up with just lately. She did give Rose her wretched part back; you've got to grant her that. She could quite easily have hung on to it – after all, she *was* the one they originally wanted. Not only that –'

Not only that, someone had just come in at the front gate. It must be Rose. Nicola sprang up from her hiding place and went to open the front door, as a person might do who had been casually coming down the stairs and just happened to be passing.

Rose looked at her, triumphantly, as she walked up the path, balancing on the cement rim which bordered it.

'Did you catch it?'

'Catch what?' said Nicola. 'Housemaid's knee?'

'Catch it for playing on the building site.'

'No. Did you expect me to?' Nicola waited until Rose had almost reached the front door. 'Stupid *tell* tale.' She thrust her face into Rose's: Rose toppled over, with a shriek, into the flower bed. 'Serves you right,' said Nicola. 'I hope you take root and get eaten by *toads*.'

8

The auditions for *The March Girls* were being held the following week, in a theatre up in London. Madam Paula had arranged for Rose and Nicola to go on Friday morning, at eleven o'clock – Mrs Bruce was to go with them, as chaperone. There hadn't been any difficulty about including Nicola. Madam Paula had been quite willing for, as she said, if she *did* happen to land herself a part it would all be added publicity for the Madam Paula Academy.

'Not to mention,' said Mr Bruce, drily, 'ten per cent of her earnings.'

Nicola couldn't imagine having earnings – even Rose had never had *earnings*. It somehow didn't seem quite real. In fact, nothing seemed quite real except for missing school on Friday. She hadn't told anyone where she was going, not even her own particular gang. Her form mistress had had to know, of course – Mrs Bruce had written a note, explaining – but her form mistress wasn't one for making a fuss or splashing bits of information around. Half the school knew where Rose was going: Nicola preferred to keep the news to herself.

On Friday morning, at half-past nine (so as to run no risk of being late) they set off for the station.

'I've told Mrs French,' said Rose, self-important, 'that she isn't to worry . . . even if I do get a part the rehearsals don't start for nearly a month. I'll still be able to play the Bad Little Girl.'

95

She shot a glance at Nicola, to see how she was taking it: Nicola preserved a stony silence. She wasn't giving Rose the satisfaction of knowing that she still had a sore place inside her.

Rose skipped happily, several paces ahead. She was wearing her pink net party dress, with white socks and black shiny leather shoes which buttoned over the instep. Over the pink dress she had on a pink tweedy coat, with a pink furry muff for her hands, while her hair was held back with a big, pink, satin bow. She looked, thought Nicola, like something off the top of a chocolate box. Nicola herself was wearing a dress of brown velvet, with bits of lace at the collar and cuffs. It was a dress she most particularly hated. She'd wanted to wear her new top (now that it had been washed and restored to its original whiteness) but Mrs Bruce wouldn't hear of it.

'Not for an *audition* . . . the aim is to make yourself look pretty.'

She couldn't see how the brown velvet dress was supposed to make her look pretty: her neck stuck out of the top of it like half a yard of broom handle, and the sleeves were about two inches too short, which made her wrists dangle. At least she had been spared the white socks. She had refused point blank. In the end, after much grumbling, Mrs Bruce had let her wear her black wool tights.

'Makes you look like little orphan Annie . . . they're not *looking* for orphans. You look like something that's come out of an institution.'

At any rate, thought Nicola, it was better than looking like something that had come off the top of a chocolate box.

'P'raps I could be a Hummel,' she said.

'What's a Hummel?' That was Rose, ignorant as usual.

'The *Hummels* . . . the poor people they take food to on Christmas morning. Where Beth catches the fever . . . don't you know *any*thing?'

Nicola had spent the last few evenings rereading *Little Women*. Rose hadn't read it at all. All she knew was that there were four leading parts, called Amy, Meg, Beth and Jo, in the first few scenes (after that, they grew up and were played by older people) and she was determined to get one of them. She wasn't interested in minor characters such as Hummels. All the way up to Victoria in the train she kept saying, 'I wonder if Susie Hamilton will be there . . . I wonder if there'll be anyone from Maude Foskett . . . I wonder if we'll see that awful girl with the squint . . . I wonder if they'll want us to dance . . . I can dance in these shoes almost as well as in my tap shoes, so it doesn't really matter if they do . . . d'you remember how awful it was in the *Annie* audition when that girl burst into tears and ran away? I wonder if anyone'll do that today? I hope they don't. It makes me feel so *awful* . . . it makes me feel really embarrassed for them.'

Never mind *Rose* feeling embarrassed: it made Nicola want to curl up and die, just listening to her. If there'd been a corridor, she'd have gone and stood in it. She tried concentrating her thoughts on things outside the window, but there wasn't any escaping Rose's voice. It filled the whole carriage.

'I wonder if the Tots Agency will send anyone . . . I wonder if we'll see that girl we saw last time . . .'

The theatre was in Shaftesbury Avenue, which meant they had to take a tube from Victoria to Green Park, and then another from Green Park to Leicester Square. Nicola liked travelling by tube. She liked looking at all the people. They were quite different from the sort of people who lived in Streatham High Road. Some of them were so strange – she saw a man with his hair in two long pigtails down to his waist, and a boy with red finger nails and lipstick – that they made Rose look quite ordinary. It was a relief, for once, to find Rose reduced to ordinariness. It seemed to subdue even her, because she actually sat in silence all the way from

Green Park to Leicester Square, a journey which must have lasted very nearly five minutes. Not until they arrived at the theatre did she regain her normal bounce.

'This is where we came before . . . that time we came for the dancing thing and they said what a pity it was I was too young else I'd have got the part.'

'That's right,' said Mrs Bruce. 'Nicola, come along and don't dawdle!'

'She's probably scared,' said Rose. 'Most people are. *I'*m not.'

'We all know you're not,' said Mrs Bruce.

'Neither am I,' said Nicola. 'I'm not scared.'

It was quite true: she wasn't. She didn't see what there was to be scared of. It was only an audition. She'd heard enough about auditions from Rose to know what to expect. You got up on a stage, with lots of other girls, and people came and looked at you, and measured how tall you were, and wrote down what colour hair you had, and what colour your eyes were, and then they asked you to do something, like sing a song or perform a little dance. Sometimes Rose had had to learn a song beforehand, or have a dance already prepared, but this time they'd been told there wasn't any need. If there had been, Nicola knew what she would have done. She'd have sung the song Miss Murray had told her off about, and she'd have sung it with the funny words – *Sleep on a wooden door, and in thy slumber snore* – and after she'd sung the word snore, she'd have put her head on her hands and made a loud snoring noise. And if she'd had to prepare a dance, she'd have done the sailor's hornpipe, which they'd learnt in PE last week when it had been raining and they'd had to stay indoors. Miss Grant had said that hers was the best hornpipe of anyone's, and that had included Janice Martin, who did ballet.

'I expect they'll give us something to improvise,' said Rose, knowledgeably. 'That's what they sometimes do.'

Nicola wasn't sure what improvise meant. She thought perhaps it might mean making things up on the spot, but she certainly wasn't going to pander to Rose's vanity by asking. She was already quite swollen-headed enough. When she had first heard that Nicola was to come to the audition with them, Rose had been inclined to flounce and be resentful. *She* was the one who went to auditions, not Nicola. What did Nicola want to come for? What was the point? She couldn't sing, she couldn't dance – it was *stupid*. Since then, her attitude had changed. It was no longer Rose resentful, but Rose benevolent, Rose patronizing – and Rose patronizing was almost harder to bear than Rose anything else. If she had told Nicola once that it would be 'all right', because everyone was always 'ever so nice to beginners', she had told her a dozen times, just as she had promised a dozen times to stand next to Nicola on stage, so that if she got lost – 'if they give us some steps to do, or anything' – she could watch what Rose was doing and pick it up from her. Now, in her bossy way, without waiting for the stage door man to give them directions, she went skipping off ahead, calling out to Nicola and her mother to follow.

'It's down here . . . I remember from last time.'

Nicola and Mrs Bruce walked sedately behind her. There were times when Nicola felt quite adult compared with Rose. Rose really was such a *child*. Always showing off and trying to attract attention.

'In here!' She flung open a door, and went prancing through into a long, narrow room with mirrors and dressing tables all down one side. 'Goody! We're first!'

Rose did an exultant pirouette before one of the mirrors. Nicola looked at her own reflection and screwed up her face: she *hated* the brown velvet dress.

'Don't do that,' said Mrs Bruce, 'it makes you look ugly. Try smiling for once.'

She smiled – and Rose giggled. Nicola sat down, with her

back to the mirror. It was just affectation, looking at oneself.

Other people started to come in; soon the room was quite crowded. Nicola thought there must be at least forty bodies in there, although half of those, of course, were mothers. She looked around at the other girls, trying to see if there were any like herself – any who *weren't* pretty and chocolate-boxish. It was a comfort to discover that there were one or two. In particular she noted a large, flabby girl with long yellow hair and a face like a horse, and a small spidery child with buck teeth. (Rose informed her, in a whisper, that 'that was the one that ran away and cried'. Rose had met most of the girls before, at other auditions. She kept waving and calling out across the room.

'Hallo, Susie! Hallo, Dominique! Hallo, Kate!'

At last, at eleven o'clock, a lady in blue dungarees appeared and checked off their names on a list. Rose, self-important, in penetrating tones, informed Nicola that 'I expect we'll all go up on stage now.'

'That's it,' said the lady. She nodded at Rose. 'I seem to recognize you . . . have you been here before?'

Rose beamed, and blossomed.

'We were here last year,' said Mrs Bruce. 'For the *Great Charlene* auditions. Unfortunately, she was a bit too young then . . . she was only nine at the time.'

'Ah, yes,' said the lady. 'I remember . . . quite a baby, weren't you?'

All the mothers and most of the girls turned to look at Rose, but they didn't look at her as people usually looked, with indulgent smiles and stupid simpers. Instead, they looked at her quite coldly, almost disapprovingly, as if she had done something wrong. It was a pity, thought Nicola, that a few more people didn't look at Rose like that. It was bad enough when she only drew attention to her*self*, but now she'd gone and drawn attention to Nicola, as well. Not that Nicola had anything against attention; not as such.

Attention was all right when you'd done something to deserve it – when you'd just turned a double back somersault in gym, or just had an essay read out by Miss McMaster (or just been told off for singing 'stupid and ridiculous' words in a singing class). What she objected to was when people stood and stared for absolutely no reason.

The mothers were all starting to bunch up together: they were going to go and sit in the auditorium and watch. As Mrs Bruce departed, she gave Nicola's hand an encouraging squeeze and whispered, 'Just do your best . . . nothing to be scared of.' Nicola wondered why everyone kept expecting her to be scared. It wasn't as if it was anything important, like exams.

The mothers disappeared, and the lady in the dungarees escorted her charges – some of them, like Rose, giggling and chattering; others, Nicola noticed, grown suddenly strained and silent – along a stone corridor and up a flight of stairs towards a swing door at the end. Another moment, and they were on stage and being told to form into a line. Nicola had never been on a stage before, except for the one at school, which was scarcely any more than a glorified platform. She was surprised at how large it was – far larger than the gym: even larger than the assembly hall – and also how dirty-looking and shabby. There were some bits of scenery dotted about, and they looked pretty dirty and shabby, as well. She couldn't quite make out what they were supposed to represent, but there was no time to study them because already things were happening.

A bald gentleman in a funny coat with fringes was walking slowly down the line followed by the lady in the dungarees and another lady, wearing baggy Turkish trousers and a floppy blouse. Every now and again the bald gentleman would stop and say 'Amy' or 'Beth', or just occasionally 'Meg' or 'Jo', and then the lady in the dungarees would make a mark on her list and hand over a

101

large white label with a letter and a number written on it. When he came to Rose, the bald gentleman hardly even bothered to look: he just said 'Amy' and passed straight on to Nicola. He looked at Nicola long and hard, through narrowed eyes, seemed about to move on, then suddenly, over his shoulder, flung an instruction at the lady in the dungarees, 'Try her as Jo.' Nicola was given a label with a big red 'J' in the middle of it, and a small black '2' in the bottom right-hand corner. The label had a loop that went over the head, and strings that tied behind. It wasn't very elegant, but anything that helped cover up the hideous velvet dress could only be good. She bet Rose wasn't too happy, having to ruin the effect of the pink net party frock.

Rose had a label with an 'A' on it, and a '4' in the corner. It seemed there were more Amys and Beths than there were Megs and Jos, because when he had reached the end of the line the bald gentleman turned to the lady in the dungarees and said, 'OK, we've got enough As and Bs; do you want to make the numbers up?' and the lady in the dungarees went back to the beginning and began handing out Js and Ms to people who hadn't been given anything first time around. Nicola was glad she wasn't one of them. She thought that it must be rather depressing, just being there to make the numbers up.

When all the labels had been allocated, they had to divide into four groups, according to which letters they were, and arrange themselves in height order; and when they'd done that, the tallest from each group had to come forward, and then the second tallest, and then the third, and so on, until in the end they had formed themselves into six different groups of four, each with a Jo, a Meg, an Amy and a Beth. Nicola had been the second tallest in her original group, while Rose had been next to bottom in hers, so fortunately they finished up in different 'families'. Nicola definitely hadn't wanted to be in the same family as Rose.

'All right, people!' The bald man in the funny coat clapped his hands for silence. 'Now, you all know what parts you're doing – right? OK. So we've got a little song here that we want you to learn – no need to look worried, it's only a few bars. It goes like this . . . *We are the March girls, We're not stiff and starch girls, We're Amy, Meg and Beth, and Jo* . . . got it? You see, it's quite simple. Let's try it with the music. Sandy! Can we have some music, please? Right! All together, now . . . *We are the March girls, We're not stiff and starch girls –*'

It took a few minutes for everyone to get it right. It wasn't that the tune was difficult, but that some people couldn't seem to remember which order the names came in, or even if they remembered they kept getting them in a muddle. Rose was one who got them in a muddle. She kept singing, 'Amy, Beg and Meth' – then clapping a hand over her mouth and giggling. When at last even Rose was able to do it without collapsing, the lady in the Turkish trousers showed them some steps which they had to do as an accompaniment.

'It's just a little march, really – the March march, as you might say – but it'll be your first entrance, so we want it to look impressive.'

The march was jolly, and swaggering. Each group came on in turn, in a line, and went swinging across the stage, heads held high, arms and legs going like pistons, as they sang their song. Nicola enjoyed it – she could have gone on marching all day. She was quite sorry when the bald man said he thought he'd seen enough, and that it was time they moved on.

'Back you go, into your original groups . . . scurry, scurry! Time is precious! We'll take the Jos first. Barbara, will you do the honours? I'll be getting on with the Megs. Amys and Beths, you can have a bit of a breather.'

The six Jos all went off into a corner with the lady in the Turkish trousers.

'Another little song,' she said. 'This is the Jo song. Not

quite as simple as the other, but I don't think you should have too much difficulty. It goes like this . . . *Jo, Jo, Jo, I wish I WERE a Jo. A REAL Jo, GO Jo, proper boyish JO Jo.'*

Nicola didn't like the Jo song. She tried telling herself that the reason she didn't like it was that Jo wouldn't ever sing anything so stupid, but she knew that it wasn't really that. The real reason she didn't like it was because she couldn't do it. It wasn't the words that defeated her so much as the tune – she simply couldn't get the notes right. She could *hear* them all right, in her head; but what she heard in her head wasn't what came out of her mouth.

When all the Jos had done their song and the bald man had listened to them, Nicola was told that she could go. All the Jos were told that they could go except for Jo 1 and Jo 3. Jo 1 was the girl called Susie Hamilton, whom Rose knew, and Jo 3 had long chestnut hair and looked exactly *like* a Jo. Nicola knew enough about auditions to know that these were the two who still stood a chance: the rest of them had been dismissed as useless. As she left the stage (not trailing or pouting like Jos 4–6: that would be showing one's feelings too much) the bald man crooked a finger at her and said: 'Jo 2! Here a minute . . . you're a nice little mover – very nice little mover. But whoever told you you could sing?'

Nicola grinned, in spite of herself.

'Nobody.'

'Nobody, eh?' The bald man grinned back at her. 'Well, I'm afraid nobody's quite right . . . you can't! You concentrate on the dancing. That's where your talent lies.'

Somehow, after that, Nicola didn't mind so much about being dismissed. After all, it was nothing new that she couldn't sing – she had *always* known that she couldn't sing. No one had ever told her before that she was a nice little mover.

The lady in the dungarees took back their labels, then led the four discarded Jos round to the auditorium to collect their chaperones. As Nicola slipped into a seat next to her mother, Mrs Bruce whispered, 'That wasn't bad at all. I thought you were quite good. Far better than that last girl.' The last girl had been the spiderlike child with the buck teeth. Nicola pulled a face.

'I can't sing.'

'Never mind. You can do other things.'

There was a pause.

'What sort of other things?' said Nicola, hopefully.

She waited for her mother to tell her that she was a nice little mover, but Mrs Bruce only clicked her tongue against the roof of her mouth and said, 'That terrible child with the yellow hair! Why *will* they let them do it? Some parents simply have no sense of responsibility.'

I don't care, thought Nicola. The bald man in the funny coat thought she was a nice little mover – a *very* nice little mover. She bet he knew more about it than Mrs Bruce.

Up on stage, four of the six Megs had just been told they could go, and one had burst into tears.

'Really!' said Mrs Bruce. 'Thank heavens Rose doesn't behave like that.'

Six Beths had now come forward and one after another were singing their Beth song. Nicola didn't take too much notice of them: she was too busy thinking about what the man in the funny coat had said. *A nice little mover . . . a VERY nice little mover . . .*

Not until it was the turn of the Amys did she sit up and pay attention. When all was said and done, Rose *was* her sister, and she supposed she *ought* to want her to do well. The Amy song might almost have been written for Rose. It went:

How fine to be pretty
And witty
And cute!
How fine to be me —
Ah me!
A-my!

Rose not only sang it with great gusto – Rose had a voice that both kept in tune *and* could be heard all over the theatre – but she also sang it in an American accent, which hardly anybody else had dared to try, or maybe they simply hadn't thought of it. Nicola had to admit that it hadn't occurred to *her*, even though she had read the book and knew perfectly well that it was set in America. She had a moment of grudging admiration for her sister. Rose might be horrid, but she could certainly do a song and dance routine.

No one was surprised when Rose was one of the two Amys asked to stay behind; and probably no one was surprised when a week later Madam Paula rang to say that Rose had been offered the part. Rose herself made a great show of pretended amazement – 'I never thought I stood a *chance* . . . Katie's so much *better* than I am . . . she's so much *prettier*' – but it didn't ring true. She was only saying it because she thought it sounded humble.

Mr French declared that they must have a celebration, and took them all up the road at Saturday lunch time for hamburgers and milk shakes at McDonald's, while Mrs French made a cake in the shape of a book and wrote *AMY* on it, in curly, icing-sugar letters. All the neighbours were told, and the local newspaper, who came round to take a photograph. Their grandparents, both lots, sent telegrams saying WHO'S A CLEVER GIRL? and WELL DONE ROSE. Even Nicola went out and bought a special *Congratulations* card and wrote 'Love from Ben and Nicola' in it. (It cost her an effort, but she was glad when she'd done it: it made her feel pleasantly generous and noble.)

On the Saturday evening, after tea, when they'd demolished half the cake and Nicola and her mother were doing the washing up – Rose having been let off, as a special treat, and Mr Bruce never doing it because of doing other things, like putting new washers on taps, and Mrs Bruce, in any case, not considering it 'man's work' – her mother suddenly said, 'Your father and I have been thinking . . .

Rose is going to be earning money, doing something that she likes doing, and I daresay we shall let her spend some of it on herself. We shan't insist that she saves every single penny of it . . . now, what about you?' She stopped, and looked at Nicola. 'Is there anything special that you would like? Anything you'd like to do? Like to buy? Anywhere you'd like to *go*?'

She was only asking her because she thought that Nicola would be feeling left out – because she didn't want her getting jealous. But she wasn't jealous. She honestly didn't care that Rose had got the part of Amy. Rose deserved it, because Rose was good at it. What Rose wouldn't be good at was the Bad Little Girl, and *that* was the only thing that Nicola wanted. She wanted her own part back again.

'Well?' said Mrs Bruce. 'There must be something!'

Nicola shook her head. She knew it wasn't any use asking for what she really wanted. They'd say it was too late, and that in any case the costumes had already been made.

'Oh, now, come on!' Mrs Bruce took a handful of cutlery out of the water. 'I can't believe there isn't *any*thing . . . how about a new bicycle?'

Politely, Nicola said, 'I like the one I've got already, thank you.'

'Well, then, how about . . . how about a portable television set for your bedroom? Then you could watch whatever you wanted.'

'I don't really like watching television,' said Nicola.

'You don't really like watching television . . . all right, then! How about taking lessons in something? Ice skating – how about ice skating? You're quite good at games and gym . . . you'd probably be a winner at ice skating.'

A thought flashed across Nicola's mind: she didn't particularly want to learn *ice* skating –

'Something else?' said Mrs Bruce.

'No,' She dismissed the idea. It had already been laughed

108

at once: she wasn't running the risk a second time. 'It's really quite all right.' Composedly, she picked up a plate from the draining board. 'You don't *have* to give me anything.'

Mrs Bruce seemed taken aback.

'I know we don't *have* to – we just thought that we'd like to. Why don't you think about it? Then if anything strikes you, you can let us know.'

'All right,' said Nicola. 'But it's not actually *necessary*.'

9

Now that she was a genuine professional (or 'pro', as she and Mrs Bruce preferred to call it) Rose had become somewhat condescending in her attitude towards the part of the Bad Little Girl. One might have thought, listening to her, that she was already a big name and really ought not to be wasting her valuable time appearing on the same stage as a bunch of mere amateurs. Needless to say, she made no move to offer the part back to Nicola. She said that she had 'given her word', and that once you'd given your word it was very important you should keep it: Madam Paula had said so.

'I couldn't let them down *now* . . . not after saying that I'd do it.'

Not after sulking and sobbing for a whole week because you thought you weren't going to be *allowed* to do it, thought Nicola, sourly.

Word had got out at school, in spite of Mr Henry's policy of not announcing individual achievements until the last day of term. Everyone knew that Rosemary Bruce had been given a part in a West End show. Some people were predictable, and gushed, 'She's ever so clever, your sister, isn't she? She must be *ever* so good.' Others, equally predictable, tried to make out that it wasn't really anything so very wonderful. Janice Martin, who did ballet, said loftily that *her* dancing teacher wouldn't let her try for 'that sort of thing', and Linda Baker, whose cousin had gold medals and had failed three times to get into the Royal Ballet School, sniffed and said, 'Of course, it's only a musical . . . *any*one can do *musicals*.' One or two, however, looked at Nicola with a mixture of sympathy and curiosity and asked her whether she didn't mind, having a sister who was going to be famous.

'I don't expect she's going to be famous, exactly,' said Nicola. 'Not playing Amy. She's only got three scenes.'

On the other hand, Rose probably *would* be famous, one of these days. She was always saying that she would be, and Nicola saw no reason to doubt her.

'She'll be *quite* famous,' said Sarah Mason, who was one of Nicola's special friends.

'She is already,' said Cheryl Walsh. Cheryl was neither friend nor foe, but stood on strictly neutral ground in between. 'Everybody's talking about her . . . I wouldn't want to have a sister that everybody talked about.'

Nicola frowned. People had always talked about Rose. She had grown used to it by now – just as she had grown used to the idea of Rose being famous.

'Wouldn't *you* like to be famous?' said Sarah.

'Not particularly,' said Nicola.

'But won't you absolutely hate it if she's famous and you're not?'

'Imagine if she keeps being on television,' said Cheryl, 'and you're stuck working in a lousy shop.'

'I'm not going to be stuck working in a lousy shop,' said Nicola.

'How d'you know?'

''Cos I know.'

'*How* d'you know?'

''Cos I'm going to be doing something else.'

'What?'

They looked at her, challengingly. Nobody in their class knew what they were going to be doing after they'd left school except for one boy who was going to be a soldier because that was what his father was. It was too far ahead for anybody else. Mostly, they hadn't even thought about it.

Nicola hadn't thought about it, either; not until that moment.

'I'm going to be a doctor,' she said.

They considered the idea.

'That'd be all right,' said Sarah. 'Then when Rose got ill through being so famous she could come and be your patient.'

Nicola tossed her head.

'I'm not having *Rose* as my patient . . . not *ever*.'

The mime show was going to have four performances in all – one in the church hall, one in an old people's home, one in a centre for the disabled, and one in a local hospital. The one in the church hall, which was the one the public were invited to, was on a Saturday evening, just two days after the end of term. Nicola couldn't make up her mind whether she wanted to go or whether she didn't. To go would be agony – but then, so would not to go. In any case, it really didn't matter a jot which way she decided, since Mrs Bruce had already decided for her.

'Of course you're coming! You can't stay at home by yourself all evening.'

'I could always go next door.'

'Go next door? What on earth for?'

'So I wouldn't have to be by myself.'

'Oh, don't be so silly, Nicola! You'll enjoy it once you're there.'

She would have enjoyed it more if she hadn't had to wear the brown velvet dress – and even *more* if she hadn't had to face the dismal prospect of watching Rose ruining her part. (She still thought of it as 'her part'; she couldn't help it. It *was* her part.)

The Family Portrait came right at the end of the programme, which meant she had it looming over her the whole of the evening. In spite of that, there were moments when she almost managed to forget it. One of those moments was in a sketch called *The Reading of the Will*, when Mr Marlowe, who had christened her Supermouse and was playing the part of an Angry Relation, banged very fiercely with his fist upon an imaginary table and then sat down with a painful *thump* on an imaginary chair which wasn't there. Nicola giggled so much that her insides began to hurt, and Mrs Bruce had to put a finger to her lips and say 'Sh!'

Another moment was when Mrs French, all by herself, did a mime called *The Awakening*. The programme didn't say what it was an awakening *of*, but explanations weren't really necessary, because anyone could see that it was a flower, gradually pushing its way up through the earth and unfolding towards the light. Nicola was quite shocked when at the end, under cover of the applause, her father leaned towards her and whispered, 'So what was all that supposed to be about?' Surely if she could see that it was a flower, then he ought to be able to? After all, he *grew* them. She tried explaining to him, but Mrs Bruce said, 'Be *quiet*, you two!' which made Mr Bruce pull a henpecked face and close one eye at Nicola in a naughty grimace.

At last it was time for *The Family Portrait*. The curtain swung back, and there was Mr Marlowe, dressed in a frock coat and funny check trousers, setting up his imaginary camera, fussily moving it from one position to another, diving under his imaginary cover to peer through the lens. And now here came all the others, just as Nicola remembered. First Papa, with a big bushy beard, then Mama, wearing a lace cap on her head, followed by Elder Brother and Sister, Nurse with the Baby, wrapped up in a white shawl, and finally, hand in hand, the Bad Little Girl and the Good Little Boy. Rose looked angelic. She looked as if butter wouldn't melt in her

113

mouth. She was wearing a buttercup yellow dress, with frilly pantaloons which peeped out beneath, and a pair of black ballet slippers decorated with rosettes the same colour as the dress. Her hair had been parted in the middle and hung enchantingly on either side of her face in bunches of ringlets. Mark, playing the Good Little Boy, was dressed in a sailor suit and long white stockings. It was hard to say which of them looked the more saintlike, him or Rose.

Nicola waited impatiently for the moment when Mama shook her finger and the Bad Little Girl had to pull a hideous face: Rose beamed, adorably, and half the audience made little crooning noises; at which Rose, ever conscious of the impression she was making, beamed even more. She knew that if she beamed long enough, she could make dimples appear in her cheeks. Nicola felt somewhat nauseated.

She waited for the next moment – the moment when the Bad Little Girl had to produce her pet mouse and let it escape. The moment came. Rose dipped a hand into her pocket and brought out something that was small and wriggly. It might have been a guinea pig, perhaps, or a kitten. What it quite definitely was not was a mouse. Nicola could see that it wasn't a mouse. It was too *big* for a mouse. Mice weren't just small, they were absolutely tiny. The thing Rose was holding was more like a teddy bear. More like an *elephant*. The elephant broke loose and went bounding like a kangaroo across the floor. Rose's ringlets bobbed violently as she followed its progress. Up and down, it went; up-and-down, up-and-down. It might almost have been a beach ball. Or a frog. It bounced as far as the Photographer, and then, quite suddenly, it disappeared. One minute it was there, and the next minute it wasn't. Perhaps it had changed into an ant, thought Nicola, and been trodden on. The audience were plainly puzzled. It wasn't until the Elder Sister screamed and jumped on to a chair with her skirts clutched round her legs that they understood what was supposed to be happening and began to laugh. Papa went marching across to the Bad Little Girl and shook her angrily by the ear; but Rose, instead of squirming and pulling a wicked I-don't-care face, only bit her lip and quivered and looked pathetic. An old lady sitting near Nicola made a sentimental cooing noise. Nicola wanted to lean across and shout, 'You aren't *meant* to feel sorry for her – she did it on *purpose*. She's *always* doing things on purpose!' It wouldn't have made any difference. The audience thought Rose was wonderful. Audiences always would; Nicola suddenly saw it, quite clearly. It didn't matter that what Rose was doing was all wrong for the part: she was being herself, and that was enough.

At the end of the show, when all the cast were lined up for their applause, Mr Marlowe stepped forward, and holding up a hand for silence said, 'Ladies and gentlemen . . . thank you for coming along on this cold night. Your support has been much appreciated. We only hope that you've enjoyed yourselves. Before you go, we thought you might be interested in a little snippet of information about one of the members of our cast . . . Miss Rosemary Vitullo.' (Rose of *course* had got her own way about changing her name.) 'Rosemary is shortly going to be starting rehearsals in the West End, no less . . . she's to play the part of the young Amy, in the musical version of *Little Women*.' He held out a hand, to a pink-cheeked Rose. 'Come along, young lady! Come and take a bow . . . no need to be shy.'

Rose was never shy. If she was pink-cheeked, it was through gratification. She stood there, dimpling, while the audience clapped and clapped. Mrs Bruce clapped as loudly as anyone. Nicola and her father clapped as well, but not quite so loudly.

'I'm sure we all wish her the very best of luck,' said Mr Marlowe. 'May it be the start of a long and illustrious career.'

Rose bowed, prettily, and stepped back into line. (Why was it, wondered Nicola, that Rose always seemed to know instinctively what to do? It didn't matter what situation she was in, so long as she had an audience she couldn't go wrong.) The curtain came down for the last time, and Mrs Bruce, with a bustle, stood up.

'Come on, then!' She handed Nicola her coat – a tweedy one, like Rose's, only brown instead of pink, to go with the brown velvet dress. 'Let's make our way backstage.'

'If you're going backstage,' said Mr Bruce, 'I'll see you outside.'

Mr Bruce didn't like having to go backstage. He didn't very much like the theatre at all. He worked as an accountant in a firm of surveyors and he liked life to be stable and ordered, as it was in his ledger books. He didn't enjoy excitement and crisis and never knowing whether tomorrow was going to be the same as yesterday. Rose and Mrs Bruce thrived on it. For her part, Nicola rather thought that she took after her father. Her school exercise books were always neat and tidy (unlike Rose's, which tended to be a sprawling mess) and she kept the books on her bedroom shelf in strict alphabetical order, becoming quite upset if ever her mother, for any reason, chanced to move them. Rose kept *her* books – not that she ever read them – all jumbled up in a heap on top of a cupboard. Probably, thought Nicola, that showed that Rose had an artistic temperament. It was probably very artistic to keep books jumbled up in heaps on the tops of cupboards, and to leave all one's things lying about, and . . .

'Come along, dozy!' Her mother gave her a little push. 'What are you dithering for?'

'I'm not dithering.'

'Well, come along, then! Let's get a move on.'

She would rather have gone to wait outside with her father, but she had left it too late: he had already

116

disappeared. She had no option but to trail backstage behind Mrs Bruce.

Backstage was in a turmoil, as usual, though it wasn't nearly as bad as after one of Madam Paula's shows. At Madam Paula's you got mothers – dozens and dozens of mothers – and half a million children, all showing off. Here, at least, it was mostly grown ups; husbands and wives and friends of the cast, with just the occasional younger person like herself. There was only one person showing off, and that was Rose, who was dashing about shrieking in her yellow dress. No one was making any attempt to check her. Even Mrs Bruce, who usually made at least a token effort, only smiled indulgently and said, in apologetic tones, to a complete stranger whose ear Rose had just shrieked down, 'She's a bit over-excited, I'm afraid'; and the complete stranger, instead of suggesting that Rose be required to keep her voice down to a more acceptable level, simply smiled back and said, 'Perfectly natural ... anyone would be, getting a part in the West End. Is she your daughter? You must be very proud of her.'

'Oh, we are,' said Mrs Bruce. 'Aren't we?'

She turned to Nicola, for confirmation.

'Yes,' said Nicola.

'We always knew she'd make it one day, but I must say we never expected it quite so soon. Did we?'

'No,' said Nicola.

'How old is she?' said the stranger.

'She was ten in October. Just thirteen months younger than my other daughter here.'

'And does your other little daughter do anything?'

'Not theatrically,' said Mrs Bruce. 'She's the clever one, aren't you, Nicola?'

'Don't know,' said Nicola.

'Of course you are! You write essays, don't you?'

Nicola picked at a button on her coat. She wished her

117

mother wouldn't. She knew she was only trying to be kind, but people didn't *want* to hear about her being clever or writing essays. They wanted to hear about Rose.

'It must all be very exciting,' said the stranger. 'Has she ever done anything professionally before? The other little one, I mean?'

While Mrs Bruce was explaining how Rose had very nearly but not quite got a part in *Annie*, and how she would have got a part in the *Great Charlene* except for being just a few months too young, Mrs French's husband appeared. He had a harassed expression on his face and a cigarette burning to nothing between his fingers. Perhaps he, too, like Mr Bruce, didn't care for coming backstage. Unlike Mr Bruce, however, he was looking extremely dashing, in black velvet jacket and trousers, with a bright red shirt and a silk scarf tied about his neck. Nicola thought he was the handsomest man she had ever seen. She smiled at him, hopefully, not really expecting him to recognize her, but he stopped, at once, and said, 'Hallo! It's the girl with the feet . . . Nicola, isn't it? That your sister they're all making eyes at?'

Nicola nodded, suddenly bashful. Mr French pulled a face.

'Don't envy you,' he said. 'Never mind . . .' He winked at her. 'Keep your pecker up!'

'Was that Mrs French's husband?' said Mrs Bruce, a few minutes later. 'What was that he was saying about feet?'

'It was just something Mrs French said.'

'Oh? What was that?'

'She said that feet were important . . . she said I had good high arches and two toes the same length.'

'Two toes the same length?'

'For point work,' said Nicola.

'But you're not going to –' Mrs Bruce broke off. 'There's the man that played the Photographer.'

119

'Mr Marlowe,' said Nicola. She wondered if he would remember her. Probably he wouldn't. People didn't always; not once they'd seen Rose.

'Someone said he used to be a professional,' said Mrs Bruce.

Mr Marlowe suddenly caught sight of Nicola, and waved. 'Hallo, Supermouse!' He blew her a kiss: Nicola blushed. 'How's Supermouse getting on?'

'All right, thank you,' said Nicola.

'Basking in reflected glory? Or aren't you the basking type?'

Nicola wasn't quite sure what he meant by that. She wrinkled her nose, uncertainly. It was Mrs Bruce who said, 'She's very happy for Rose. Aren't you?'

'Yes,' said Nicola.

'I should hope we all are,' said Mr Marlowe. He chucked Nicola under the chin. 'Attaboy, Supermouse! Keep up the good work!'

'Strange man,' said Mrs Bruce, as soon as Mr Marlowe was out of earshot.

'He's nice,' said Nicola.

'What's all this about Supermouse?'

'That's what he called me,' said Nicola. 'Because of –'

She had been going to say, 'Because of me doing such a good mouse,' but fortunately, perhaps, Mrs French arrived in time to stop her. (It wouldn't have been the right thing to say at this particular moment. Tonight was Rose's night: no one wanted to hear about Nicola.) She listened, patiently, as Mrs Bruce related yet again the story of the audition, explaining how Rose had come to get the part, and what a wonderful thing it was for her career. She heard Mrs French agree that it was, indeed, wonderful for Rose's career, and Mrs Bruce say that of course it was only the first rung on the ladder, and Mrs French say that everyone had to start somewhere, and Mrs Bruce say that Rose had been

120

extremely lucky, and Mrs French say that she had indeed, and Mrs Bruce say that they were thinking, after *The March Girls*, of sending her to a full-time stage school, and could Mrs French perhaps recommend any? Madam Paula had suggested the Italia Conti or Barbara Speke. What did Mrs French think? Mrs French said she thought that either would be perfectly splendid. She couldn't really make any other recommendations. She didn't know that much about stage schools; only ballet schools. But she was quite sure that both the Italia Conti and Barbara Speke were thoroughly reputable. What one had to avoid were the one-horse establishments which operated from two rooms and a cupboard in the back streets of suburbia.

'Oh, we shouldn't dream of letting her go to one of those,' said Mrs Bruce. 'We shall check most carefully. After all, it is her career.'

'Exactly.' There was a pause, and Nicola thought that Mrs French was going to move on; but then, suddenly, she heard her say, 'Well! That seems to be Rose taken care of . . . now, what are we going to do about Nicola?'

'Nicola?'

Mrs Bruce sounded as startled as Nicola was.

'I always hate to see good talent go to waste,' said Mrs French. 'Of course, I do realize that Nicola thinks ballet is wet, and that she far prefers a game of football –'

Nicola, who up until now had kept her eyes fixed firmly on the ground, risked a quick glance and found to her surprise that Mrs French was smiling. She had thought, after the things she had said on the building site, that Mrs French wouldn't ever want to talk to her again.

'Oh, Nicola's football mad,' said Mrs Bruce.

No, I'm not, thought Nicola. I'm not football *mad*.

Mrs French laughed.

'I'm sure there's nothing wrong with football – my husband tells me it's an excellent game. *He* says it beats *Swan*

121

Lake into a cocked hat any day of the week. I suppose it's always possible that Nicola might agree with him.' She raised a quizzical eyebrow in Nicola's direction. 'The only trouble is, there's not really very much future in it, is there? Not for a girl. Not even in this day and age. You're hardly very likely to end up playing centre forward for England!'

'Are you saying –' Mrs Bruce spoke hesitantly '– that she's any more likely to end up dancing *Swan Lake* for –' she spread out her hands '– the Royal Ballet?'

'Well, it's far too early to make predictions, of course, but . . . I always believe in giving things a go; don't you?'

Mrs Bruce puckered her lips.

'You're suggesting she should take classes? I suppose, perhaps, Madam Paula –'

'Not Madam Paula.' Mrs French spoke quickly. 'Not that she isn't excellent, in her way, but – not for Nicola. I was rather wondering whether you would let Nicola come to me.'

'To you?'

'For classes. I thought maybe just twice a week, to begin with, until we see how she develops –'

'Forgive me,' said Mrs Bruce, 'but I was under the impression you didn't take younger people?'

'I don't, as a rule. But just occasionally I make exceptions. I'd very much like to make one now, if Nicola was agreeable.'

Mrs Bruce looked down at Nicola, dubiously. Nicola's heart was pounding so hard she could hear the blood roaring in her ears.

'You really think that *Nicola* – ?'

'I think she has potential. At this stage one can't say very much more than that. But she's exactly the right build, she's supple, she's musical –'

'Musical?' said Mrs Bruce. She laughed, a trifle nervously. Nicola could understand her bewilderment. Perhaps, after all, Mrs French was only teasing?

122

'Very musical,' said Mrs French. 'The one night she was with us she picked up several quite complicated cues with no difficulty at all. Rose, of course, has been doing it all her life; but for someone who's had no training . . . mind, I'm not necessarily saying that she'd end up as a leading ballerina. She might not even make it as far as the corps – she might not even *want* to make it. She might decide she wants to do something quite different. On the other hand, she could turn out to be a second Pavlova. We just don't know until we've tried. But either way, it would seem a pity if she was never given the chance to find out.'

'Yes. Well –' Mrs Bruce seemed slightly bludgeoned. 'Perhaps if we could talk it over and let you know?'

'By all means. But the sooner the better – she's just at the right age. I wouldn't want to leave it any longer. Another few months and it would really be too late.'

'I see.' Mrs Bruce shifted her bag from one hand to the other. 'Well, in that case . . . if we could let you know first thing Monday morning?'

'Monday morning would be fine. I'll look forward to hearing from you.'

With another smile at Nicola – who this time, rather shyly, smiled back – Mrs French went on her way. There was a moment's silence, then: 'We'd better collect Rose,' said Mrs Bruce. 'Your father will be wondering what's happened to us.'

Rose was still running about shrieking in her yellow dress.

'Go and get changed,' said Mrs Bruce. 'And make it quick . . . we'll wait for you outside.'

Slowly, Nicola and her mother walked back down the passage that led to the exit.

'Well, I suppose, if you really wanted to,' said Mrs Bruce. She stopped. '*Do* you really want to?'

'Wouldn't mind,' said Nicola.

'You'd rather have ballet lessons than ice skating?'

She hunched a shoulder.

123

'What does that mean?' said Mrs Bruce. 'Yes? Or no? There'd be no point in doing it if you weren't going to enjoy it. Do you think you *would* enjoy it?'

''Spect I might.'

'You're not just saying that because you think you've got to please Mrs French? We don't want you pushed into doing something against your will – any more than we want to waste money on something that's not going to give you any pleasure. But if you're really quite sure –' She waited a moment. 'If you really do think that you'd like to try it –'

'Might just as well,' said Nicola. Even if she *was* going to be a doctor. There wasn't any harm in just trying.

'Well, I'll go round first thing Monday morning, then,' said Mrs Bruce.

Mr Bruce was pacing up and down outside the church with his hands behind his back. He turned, as he saw his wife and Nicola.

'You've taken your time. Everyone making a fuss of Rose, I suppose.'

'And of Nicola,' said Mrs Bruce. 'It appears we've got two gifted daughters . . . Mrs French wants her to go and take dancing lessons with her – seems to think she's going to be another Anna Pavlova.'

'Is that so?' said Mr Bruce. 'Well, and who knows?' He ruffled Nicola's hair, affectionately. 'Maybe she will.'

Maybe I will, thought Nicola. Not that she was going to be a dancer, she was going to be a doctor; but still, there couldn't be any harm in just *trying*.

A voice came piping from somewhere behind them, 'Who's going to be another Anna Pavlova?'

'Nicola,' said Mrs Bruce. 'Not you.'

'*Nicola?*' said Rose. She giggled.

Just for that, thought Nicola, I jolly well *will*.

That is, of course, if she didn't decide to become a doctor.

ABOUT THE AUTHOR

Jean Ure lives in London and is married to an actor, whom she met when they were both training at the Webber-Douglas School of Dramatic Art. Her first book was published while she was still at school. She has been a full-time writer since the early 1970s.

A PROPER LITTLE NOORYEFF and IF IT WEREN'T FOR SEBASTIAN . . . are published in Puffin Plus, for older readers.

Heard about the
Puffin Club?

. . . it's a way of finding out more about Puffin books and authors, of winning prizes (in competitions), sharing jokes, a secret code, and perhaps seeing your name in print! When you join you get a copy of our magazine, *Puffin Post*, sent to you four times a year, a badge and a membership book.

For details of subscription and an application form, send a stamped addressed envelope to:

The Puffin Club Dept A
Penguin Books Limited
Bath Road
Harmondsworth
Middlesex UB7 0DA

and if you live in Australia, please write to:

The Australian Puffin Club
Penguin Books Australia Limited
P.O. Box 257
Ringwood
Victoria 3134